yes, i know the
Monkey Man

yes, i know the
Monkey Man

DORI HILLESTAD BUTLER

PEACHTREE
ATLANTA

Published by
PEACHTREE PUBLISHERS
1700 Chattahoochee Avenue
Atlanta, Georgia 30318-2112

www.peachtree-online.com

Text © 2009 by Dori Hillestad Butler

Jacket design by Maureen Withee
Book design by Melanie McMahon Ives

Manufactured in United States of America

10 9 8 7 6 5 4 3 2 1
First Edition

Library of Congress Cataloging-in-Publication Data

Butler, Dori Hillestad.
  Yes, I know the monkey man / written by Dori Hillestad Butler. -- 1st ed.
     p. cm.
  Sequel to: Do you know the monkey man?
  Summary: Thirteen-year-old TJ tries to cope with the emotional upheaval in her life when the father who kidnapped her ten years earlier and raised her under a different identity is injured and she goes to visit her recently discovered twin sister, mother, and future stepfather.
  ISBN 978-1-56145-479-2 / 1-56145-479-6
  [1. Twins--Fiction. 2. Sisters--Fiction. 3. Family--Fiction. 4. Emotional problems--Fiction. 5. Identity--Fiction.] I. Title.
  PZ7.B9759Ye 2009
  [Fic]--dc22
                                        2008036748

For all the kids who read
Do You Know the Monkey Man?
and then wrote me to find out what happens next...

Chapter One

The little red light on our answering machine was blinking on and off when I wandered into the kitchen. I groaned. I could guess who that was.

"Hey, Sherlock!" I whistled for my dog. "Do you need to go outside?" It was eight o'clock in the morning, so of course he needed to go outside. He came running, tail wagging and nails clicking against our cracked kitchen floor.

"Here you go," I said, holding the back door open for him.

I wondered if we had anything for breakfast. I pressed PLAY on the answering machine and wandered over to the fridge to see what was inside. Not much. A little bit of milk. Bologna. Leftover pizza.

The machine beeped and I heard, "Hello? T.J.?" My fingers tightened around the fridge handle. "This is Sam. Again." I could tell she was trying to sound friendly and unconcerned, but she also sounded nervous. What did *she* have to be nervous about? She wasn't the one who'd had her whole life turned upside down.

"My mom and I just wanted to make sure you're still coming on Wednesday," Sam went on. "Are you? Did you get the money for the bus ticket? We need to know what bus you're coming on and what time it gets in so we can come pick you up. Could you maybe call us back and let us know?"

I grabbed the pizza box, then slammed the fridge closed.

"Oh!" I jumped when I saw Joe standing on the other side of the fridge door. He had on an old T-shirt and ratty jeans. Work clothes.

"Hey," he said as though it was just another normal day, and we were just another normal father and daughter about to sit down to a nice, delicious breakfast together. Right. I'd have gone back to my room if Sherlock hadn't still been outside. Believe it or not, Joe was the one who'd gotten me the dog. He chose a Westie because that's what he had when he was a kid. He told me Westies were smart, loyal, and independent. Which was true. Too bad everything else he'd ever told me was a lie.

"Are you planning to eat that pizza or are you just going to carry it around for a while?" Joe asked.

Very funny.

"Is there enough pizza left for both of us?" Joe tried again.

I shoved a bunch of dirty dishes aside so I could set the box on the counter. "Open it and see," I told Joe. It was the most I'd said to him in about three days.

He pulled up the lid and grabbed a slice from the pepperoni side of the pizza. Once he moved out of the way, I

2

helped myself to a slice of the bacon and pineapple and stuffed the pointy end into my mouth. It was like biting into cold cardboard. Fortunately, I happened to like cold, cardboardy pizza.

"I take it you still haven't called Sam back," Joe said as he leaned against the stove.

"Obviously not," I said, wishing my dog would hurry up. I went over to the door to wait for him.

"How many times has she called in the last couple of weeks? Three? Four?"

"More like five or six."

Joe sighed. "T.J., you have to call her back."

"Why?" Even more important, why did he care whether I called her back?

"Because when someone calls and leaves a message, you call them back. That's the way it works."

Maybe in normal families.

"I don't have enough money for the bus ticket anymore, remember?" I said. I'd given him some of the money Suzanne sent me so he could pay our electric bill. Not that I minded. If I didn't have money for the bus ticket, I wouldn't be able to go to Iowa. Oh, well.

"I've got your money right here," Joe said, reaching into his front pocket. He pulled out a wad of bills and brought them over to me.

I eyed the cash, but didn't take any. "Where'd you get all that?" I asked.

"Hey, I've got a job now, remember?" Joe said, a little too cheerfully. He grabbed my free hand, the one that didn't have the half-eaten slice of pizza in it, pressed the bills against my palm, then closed my fingers around them.

I popped the last of my pizza into my mouth and counted the money while I chewed. Twenty, forty, sixty, eighty, one hundred dollars. I'd actually given him a hundred and twenty dollars, but whatever. It wasn't my money. It was Suzanne's.

"What's the matter, T.J.?" Joe asked. "Don't you want to go to your mom's?"

Of course I didn't want to go. I didn't know these people. I didn't even know Sam and Suzanne existed until Sam showed up on our doorstep three weeks ago and said she was my sister. My twin sister. I might have been able to get excited about that under other circumstances. Like, if her existence didn't prove that my entire life had been a lie. Now I was supposed to forget everything I'd ever been told about who I was and be like any other divorce kid. Go to Iowa. Go to Suzanne's wedding and act like her daughter. It was too much. Too much, too soon.

"It'll be okay," Joe said as he went to the fridge and took out a can of Coke. "It's only a week. It'll go fast."

Was that supposed to make me feel better?

"Maybe I'll get there and decide I don't want to come back," I said, just to see what he'd say. "Did you ever think of that?"

Joe popped the tab on his Coke can. "I *have* thought of that," he said, not meeting my eyes. "And if that's what you want..." His voice trailed off.

It wasn't what I wanted.

Sherlock let out a short bark, so I let him in. He went straight to his food bowl, which was still empty. Holding tight to the hundred bucks, I grabbed the bag of dog food from the shelf next to the back door. Three ants crawled out from behind the bag. Gram would have a fit if she knew there were ants in her house. I smashed them with the bag, then poured some food into Sherlock's bowl. He nosed his way in before I even finished pouring.

"I called the bus station last night," Joe said suddenly.

I lifted an eyebrow. "*You* called the bus station?"

"Don't give me your lip. Of course I called the bus station. I knew you hadn't done it. And I thought it was about time we made a plan for Wednesday. There's a bus that leaves here at 7:20 a.m. and gets in to Cedar Rapids around 6:30 p.m. Cedar Rapids is the closest town to Clearwater that has a bus station." He looked pretty proud of himself for finding out all that information. "Why don't you call Sam back and tell her you'll be on that bus?"

"You're the one who called the bus station," I said. "Why don't *you* call her?"

Joe scratched his ear. "I don't think that would be a good idea. Do you?"

No, probably not. After everything that had happened, Joe and Suzanne had been communicating through Mrs. Morris, my social worker. It was better that way. Safer. Personally, I thought it was safer for me to communicate with Suzanne and Sam through Mrs. Morris, too, but Mrs. Morris wanted me to talk to them directly.

And now even Joe wanted me to talk to them directly.

5

He grabbed the phone and held it out to me. "Call and tell them you're coming, Teej," he said. "Please."

I stared at the phone for a couple of seconds, then went to put the bag of dog food back on the shelf. "I think we should call and tell them I'll come in a few weeks," I said. "After the wedding."

I'd never actually been to a wedding before, but I'd seen enough of them on TV to know that this was a really stupid time for my first visit. It's not like Suzanne and I would have any time to "get to know each other." Not with some big wedding going on. And then the day after the wedding they're going to be busy moving into their new house. Who invites a total stranger to their wedding and then asks the person to help them move?

"Suzanne told Mrs. Morris that she wanted both her daughters there for her wedding," Joe said. "I'm not really in a position to tell her no, am I?"

Probably not. Because if he gets on Suzanne's bad side, he could end up in jail.

Joe held the phone out to me again. "Would you please just tell them you're coming? You don't want that social worker to come over here and start nosing around again, do you?"

Of course I didn't, so I took the phone. I knew Joe would stand there until I made the call, so I went over to the answering machine, rewound the tape, and got Suzanne and Sam's phone number. My finger shook as I punched in the numbers. If I was lucky, no one would answer.

Two rings…three rings…four rings…*click*. "You have reached the Wright residence." *Yes! An answering machine.* "We can't come to the phone right now, but if you'll leave your name and number, we'll get back to you as soon as possible."

"Hi. This is—" I had to stop and think. I was T.J. As far as I was concerned, that was my name.

But *they*—Suzanne and Sam—knew me as Sarah.

Well, tough. "This is T.J.," I said. "My bus gets in to Cedar Rapids at 6:30 on Wednesday night. See you then." I hung up and handed the phone back to Joe.

He winced.

"What?" I asked.

"You could've been a little friendlier."

Considering none of this was my idea, or my fault, I could've been a lot *un*friendlier.

Chapter Two

I 'll pick you up after softball today," Joe said as he packed two peanut butter sandwiches, a bag of chips, and a Coke into his lunch box.

I unwrapped a square of grape bubble gum and popped it into my mouth. "I'll take the bus," I said between chews.

"Don't be difficult. You know your coach doesn't like it when you take the bus."

"My coach needs to get a life," I said. What did he think was going to happen to me on the 4:44 bus anyway?

Joe grunted. "I agree. But what if that social worker has been talking to him? Do you really want your mom to find out I let you take the bus by yourself?"

I shrugged. There were worse things she could find out.

"If I pick you up, we can go visit Gram afterwards," Joe said. "You do want to see Gram before you leave on Wednesday, don't you?"

I'd been planning to go see her anyway. On the bus. Just like I did every Monday, Wednesday, and Friday since she went into the nursing home.

Joe made me promise I wouldn't tell Gram about Sam showing up three weeks ago. He didn't even want me to tell Gram that I was going to visit Sam and Suzanne. He said it would confuse and upset her. I didn't want to confuse or upset her, so I kept my mouth shut. It was hard, though. My whole life, no matter where Joe and I were living, no matter what was going on, Gram was the one I called when we were in trouble or if I needed something. She told me what to do when I got my period for the first time; she told me what to do when Joe got sick and when he got arrested; she even took us in two years ago when things got really bad. She made Joe go to rehab and she took care of me, even though she was already starting to get a little forgetful. Gram had always been my safety net, but now I had to go it alone.

"We can pick up Chinese on the way home and watch the Twins game while we eat," Joe went on. "What do you say?"

"I say, what's the occasion?" Chinese food was expensive. We normally only got it for special occasions.

Joe walked over to me. "The occasion is you're leaving in two days, and I'm going to miss you," he said, cupping my chin in his hand. "I want us to do something special before you go."

Why? In case I didn't come back? I *was* coming back!

Whatever. If it was that big of a deal to him…"Practice is over at 4:30," I said. "Don't be late."

"I won't," Joe said.

Right. Joe was always late. That's why I started riding the bus.

* * *

Big surprise. It was 4:45 and no Joe. Thunder rumbled in the distance, and I gazed up at the greenish purple clouds that drifted slowly across the sky. It was growing darker by the minute.

Great. I'd just missed the 4:44 bus and there wouldn't be another bus until 5:10. I sure hoped Joe was really coming.

I leaned against the chain-link fence and lazily swung my gym bag back and forth in front of me while Monica and Megan Hayes ran around picking up all the bases, stray balls, and other equipment. Their dad, who was our coach, was jotting last-minute notes on his clipboard. Everyone else had already left.

Monica and Megan were identical twins. Like me and Sam. Funny, I'd never noticed how many twins were out there until I met Sam. The only twins I'd ever paid attention to were the Minnesota Twins, as in the baseball team. Now I saw them all over the place. Monica and Megan were an especially annoying set. Everything about them was, well...*identical.* Not just their looks, but the stuff they did for fun, their friends, everything. Was that what most twins were like?

Would Sam and I be like that if we had grown up together?

I doubted it. The only thing we had in common was our parents.

Coach Hayes shoved his clipboard in one of the duffel bags and zipped it up while his clone daughters zipped the other. "Is your dad on his way, T.J.?" he asked as the three of them strode toward me. They were such a perfect family. Perfect dad and perfect kids. I'll bet when Coach Hayes says he's going to pick Monica and Megan up from the mall at a certain time, he does it.

"Probably," I said. But who knew?

Thunder rumbled again. Louder this time. Streetlights up and down Washburn Avenue clicked on.

"Have you called him?"

"Uh, I don't have a cell phone," I said.

The clones looked at me like, *how could you not have a cell phone?* But hey, cell phones cost money. And unlike the rest of the world, we didn't have a money tree growing outside our house.

Coach unclipped his phone from his belt and held it out to me. "Use mine," he said. "If your dad can't get here in the next couple of minutes, I'll just take you home."

Monica and Megan glanced at each other out of the corners of their eyes. I could tell they didn't want to give me a ride. Let's just say the three of us didn't hang out with the same people.

"That's okay," I said. I didn't need a ride from them or anyone else. "I'm sure my dad will be here any minute." *And if he's not, I'll run down and catch the 5:10 bus.*

"Well, I can't leave you here by yourself," Coach said. "And I can't wait around much longer. So why don't you call and see what's going on?" He handed me the phone.

I had to stop and think what Joe's phone number was. He only got a phone a couple of months ago when he started working for Floyd Construction. I punched in a number I thought was Joe's and put the phone to my ear.

A loud clap of thunder sounded right above us. Large drops of rain plunked against my arms and dotted the sidewalk.

Monica and Megan shrieked in unison, then took off toward a black Toyota that was parked across the street. Coach touched my elbow. "Come on, T.J. Let's go." Rain poured down all around us.

Still holding the coach's cell phone to my ear, I hoisted my gym bag up onto my other shoulder and hurried after him. My feet slapped against the wet pavement and my toes squished inside my sopping wet socks.

"Hello? Joe?" I said once the voice mail kicked in. "Softball got out like twenty minutes ago. Where are you? Coach Hayes won't let me wait by myself, so he's going to bring me home. I'll see you there."

The clones had left the back door of the Toyota open for me, so I crawled in and the coach slammed the door closed behind me as the rain poured down even harder. It sounded like marbles rolling across the roof of the car.

"Did you get ahold of your dad?" Coach Hayes asked once he was settled in the front seat.

"Yeah," I lied. "He's stuck in traffic. The rain, you know." I handed him his phone. "He said to tell you thanks for bringing me home."

I shook the water out of my hair. The clone who was maybe Megan leaned way away from me like I was spraying germs all over her.

"So, where do you live, T.J.?" Coach asked as he stuck his key in the ignition. The air conditioning came on full blast.

Goose bumps popped out on my arms and I shivered. "Over on Sheridan," I said, rubbing my arms. "Sheridan and 74th."

"That's not too far," Coach said.

Hugging my gym bag to my chest, I leaned back against my seat and watched the little rivers of rain run along my window. The clones carried on some dumb conversation about who'd said what to whom the whole way to my house. Fine with me. That way I didn't have to talk to them. Gram was always trying to get me to make friends with the girls at school. That's why she made me join band and softball and anything else I could stand to be in for ten seconds. She didn't get that I just didn't fit in. But so what? I had Joe and Gram, and Nick and Dave next door, and my dog. That was enough.

"Which house is it?" Coach asked as he turned onto my street.

"That brown one on the left up there," I said. "The one with the broken garage window." Joe had promised Gram he'd fix that when he got out of rehab and he still hasn't done it. But then again, Gram's not here to know that he hasn't done it.

By the time we pulled into the driveway, the worst of the storm had passed. Just a light rain was falling now. "Thanks for the ride," I said, reaching for the door handle.

"No problem."

Coach waited while I walked up to my house and unlocked the front door. As soon as I did, Sherlock lunged at my knees and wagged his tail in greeting.

I smiled. "Hey, boy," I said, bending to pick him up. I held my dog in one arm, waved to Coach with the other hand, then nudged the door closed with my foot. At least he didn't come in and make sure I wasn't alone in my house. I guess he wasn't worried that someone might break into my house and kidnap me. He only worried about something happening to me on the 4:44 bus.

Sherlock wiggled around in my arms and licked my face. I kissed him on his nose and he licked me even more.

"Is Joe here?" I asked my dog as I carried him past two overflowing baskets full of laundry into the kitchen. I doubted it. The house felt empty. And I didn't see Joe's wallet or keys on the counter.

I checked the answering machine. No blinking red light.

Well, if he couldn't even leave me a message telling me where he was, why should I wait around for him? I put my dog down and grabbed the leash from the hook by the back door. Sherlock went totally nuts, leaping against my legs and running all around me.

"Yeah, you need a walk, don't you, boy?" I said as I snapped the leash to his collar and gave his head a quick rub.

I checked the clock on the microwave on our way out: 5:15.

We took a quick jog around the block, splashing through every puddle along the way. Then we loped over to the

14

park across the street. Usually when Sherlock and I run around in the park, Nick or Dave comes over with one of their dogs. But their house looked pretty dark. They probably weren't home.

I wished we had a real dog park around here. Sherlock likes to run free, but I didn't dare let him off his leash completely. He might take off for Penn Avenue and get hit by a car. So I just let his leash go and ran with him a little bit. That way if he got away and didn't come when I called, I could catch him by jumping on his leash. But he stayed right with me today. He was getting better about that.

The storm had cooled things down. It actually felt kind of nice outside now. The trees dripped water, but the sun was trying to poke through the clouds again. After half an hour of chasing sticks and squirrels, Sherlock was ready to go home. So we walked back across the street and went in the house.

Joe still wasn't home.

I kicked off my shoes, peeled off my wet clothes, and changed into dry ones. It was almost six thirty and I was starving. I had a feeling the Chinese food wasn't coming, so I stuck a frozen burrito in the microwave. While it spun on the carousel, I poured food into Sherlock's bowl. The microwave dinged, and I took my dinner into the den and turned on the TV. The game would be starting soon. Where was Joe? I'd really believed him when he said he'd pick me up at softball and we'd do something special tonight.

I peered out the window. I didn't see or hear our truck rumbling down the street.

Had he gone to see Gram without me? Had he forgotten we were going to go see her together? Or... *had something happened to Gram?* Oh no! Why hadn't I thought of that before? I picked up the phone and quickly punched in the number for the nursing home.

Someone picked up on the second ring. "Valley View. This is Kari. How can I help you?" Kari was one of the nice nurses.

"Hi," I said, gripping the phone with both hands. "This is T.J. You know, Eva Wright's granddaughter?" I waited, but Kari didn't say anything about Gram being rushed to the hospital or anything. So I said, "I was wondering if my dad was there?"

Kari paused. "No, he's not, T.J.," she said. "In fact, he hasn't been in at all tonight. That's a little unusual, isn't it?"

"A little," I said. Joe wasn't the most reliable guy in the world, but he was pretty reliable about visiting Gram. He visited her twice a day. Once on his way to work and once on his way home. Half the time Gram doesn't remember the last time someone visited, even if it was just ten minutes ago. But he still visits her twice a day anyway.

"Can I talk to my grandma?" I asked.

"Sure. Hang on." It took a while for Kari to take the phone to my grandma.

"Is it Joseph?" I heard Gram ask Kari.

"No, it's your granddaughter," Kari told her.

There was a shuffling on the phone, then Gram came on the line. "Hello? T.J.?" she said in a gravely voice.

"Hi, Gram."

"Where's your dad? Where's Joe?" I had to hold the phone away from my ear because she talked so loud.

"I...don't know. He's got a big job right now." She always forgot he had a job. "I think he's working late. He might not be able to see you tonight, but he'll be there tomorrow. I promise."

"Something's happened," Gram said suddenly.

"No—"

"Yes," Gram insisted. "Something's happened. That's why he's not here." She sounded a little freaked out. She got that way sometimes.

"Listen, Gram." I scratched the top of my head. "Do you want me to come see you?" I could probably still catch a bus over there if it would make her feel better.

There was a shuffling sound on the phone again. Then a thud.

"Hello? Gram, are you still there?"

Nothing.

"Hello!" I said louder. I pounded my hand against the phone, even though I knew that whatever was wrong wasn't in the phone. "HELLO? IS ANYONE THERE?"

"I'm sorry, T.J." It was Kari again. "Your grandma doesn't want to talk anymore."

"Is she okay? Should I come down there?"

"No. She wants your dad. She'll be going to bed soon, though. She'll be fine."

"Okay," I said, hanging up.

I looked out the window again. Still no truck.

I even went outside and jogged down the driveway.

Sherlock didn't like that I'd left him in the house. I could hear him barking at me.

"I'll be back in a minute," I told him. Then I walked down to 76th Street to see if I could spot Joe's truck getting off the freeway. I saw a blue truck turn onto Penn Avenue, but it wasn't rusty enough to be Joe's. I stood there watching the cars and trucks and minivans for what felt like half an hour, but in reality it was probably only about ten minutes. Then I slowly dragged myself back home.

Sherlock had his little paws up on the screen door when I got there. He woofed when he saw me walking up the driveway. I went inside, picked him up, and carried him back to the den.

I didn't even care about the game anymore.

Where was Joe?

At 8:45, the phone rang. I picked it up. "Hello?"

"Finally! You're home," a strange man's voice said. "Is this Joseph Wright's daughter?"

Joseph Wright's daughter? "Yes," I said carefully. "Who's this?"

"You don't know me, but my name is Russell Teagues. I'm the contractor who hired your father."

The phone grew slippery in my hand. "Uh-huh," I said, gripping the phone tighter.

"I've tried calling you a couple of times this afternoon and this evening, but I didn't want to leave a message. I wanted to tell you directly."

Tell me what?

"I'm afraid I have some bad news." The man paused. "Your dad was involved in an accident today."

My throat closed.

"We were shingling a roof over on 16ᵗʰ Street, and I don't exactly know what happened...but somehow he slipped."

"He slipped off the roof?" I felt sick. Really sick.

"Yes. He was taken to Fairview Southdale hospital."

"I-is he okay?" I asked.

"I don't know——"

"What do you mean you don't know?" I shrieked.

"He's in the hospital. It looks pretty bad."

Oh, God.

"D-do you have someone to take you to the hospital? And someone to stay with you tonight? I know it's just the two of you; I could maybe make a few phone calls——"

"No," I stopped him right there. "I mean yes. Of course, I have someone to stay with me, and someone to take me to the hospital." The last thing I needed was some stranger making a bunch of phone calls. I had the MTC bus driver to take me to the hospital, and I had my dog to stay with me overnight.

I didn't need anyone else.

Chapter Three

The first thing I had to do was find out just how badly Joe was hurt, so I headed over to the hospital. Unfortunately, it was almost nine o'clock. There weren't many buses running this time of night, but I walked along 76th Street instead of the side streets, just in case one came rumbling along behind me.

As I walked, I replayed everything Russell Teagues had said over and over inside my head. Accident...slipped off the roof...Fairview Southdale Hospital...pretty bad...

What did pretty bad mean?

A broken neck? Something with his head? Whatever it was, Joe wasn't going to...to *die* or anything, was he? He couldn't die. Not now.

As I got close to the Hennepin County Library, I saw a brief gap in traffic along York Avenue, so I darted across the first two lanes, then ran along the median until it was safe to cross the last two lanes. I kept running, as hard as I could, all the way across the Target parking lot. My arms and legs ached. My lungs burned. But I didn't slow down.

I thought about how when I was little, I used to worry about Joe dying. He always told me my real parents had died (before I found out *he* was my real parent), so I thought that if my real parents could die, then he could die, too.

"I'm not going to die, T.J.," he promised.

But everybody dies sometime.

Some guy honked at me as I zipped across 66th Street. I flipped him the bird and kept right on going. I was almost to the hospital now.

I scrambled up a small grassy hill next to the road, crossed another parking lot, speed-walked past a couple of office buildings, and finally, I found myself panting outside the hospital's emergency entrance.

The door whooshed open as soon as I stepped on the mat and a cold blast of air conditioning hit me when I walked inside. The dimly lit lobby was practically deserted. An older woman dressed in a pink smock sat at an information desk in the corner. She had her nose buried in a thick paperback.

I walked over to her and pounded my hand on the counter to get her attention. "My dad's in here somewhere," I said, trying to catch my breath. "But I don't know where he's at. I don't know what room."

"Is he a patient here?" she asked.

"Yes!" Didn't I just say that?

The lady slid her chair over a few feet and parked herself in front of a computer. "Patient's name?" she asked.

"Joseph Wright," I said, my foot tapping against the wall.

She typed something on the computer, then squinted at her screen. "Looks like he's in ICU, bed 5."

"ICU? What's that?"

"The Intensive Care Unit."

My foot stopped tapping. "Is that bad?" It sounded bad.

The lady smiled uneasily. "I don't know. If he's in ICU, that means he's being monitored."

"Monitored for what? What's wrong with him?"

"I can't answer that. You'll have to speak to his doctor. Or maybe your mother should speak to the doctor. Is she with you?"

"No," I said. "There is no mother." Not one who counted at a time like this, anyway. "There's just me."

"Oh. Well, why don't you take the elevator over there to the third floor? Turn right and go through the double doors. That's ICU. The nurses up there can help you."

"Okay. Thanks." I dashed over to the elevator and pushed the button. I pushed it three times before the doors finally opened. A guy around my dad's age was already in there. He wore tan shorts and a white shirt, and carried a huge bouquet of daisies and some other white and pink flowers. He smiled when I stepped into the elevator. I smiled back and moved to the other side of the car.

I watched the numbers on the panel above the door light up as we passed each floor. The elevator dinged when it stopped at the third floor. I got out and turned to the right, but when I got to the double doors, I stopped. There was a sign with big black letters posted on the door: Intensive Care Unit. Absolutely no live plants or flowers beyond this point.

Whoa. Were some people so sick they couldn't have flowers? Was Joe that sick?

22

Oh, no. I massaged my forehead. This wasn't happening.

"Excuse me? Can I help you?"

I turned to the nurse who had come up behind me. She was big. In fact, she was so big her smock was sort of bursting at the seams. But she looked at me with such concern that I wanted to melt.

"I-I'm here to see my dad." My voice sounded small and wobbly even to my ears.

"Is he in intensive care?" the nurse asked.

I nodded, not trusting my voice.

"What's his name?"

"Joe," I choked out. "Joseph Wright." My bottom lip trembled.

"Oh, child," the nurse said, wrapping her arms around me. I let myself fall into her because it felt so nice. Like falling into a nice warm bed and then being covered with a huge, fluffy comforter fresh out of the dryer.

"It's okay," she said, patting my back.

I will not cry...I will not cry... I bit down hard on my lip and blinked back the tears that welled in my eyes. I *never* cried. But the way that nurse kept patting my back made me want to. I pulled away from her.

"Do you know my dad?" I wiped the back of my hand across my nose. "Is he in there?" I nodded toward the double doors.

The nurse reached into her pocket and pulled out a small package of tissues. I shook my head when she offered one. I just wanted to find my dad.

"He's in there," she said, stuffing the package of tissues back into her pocket. "But he's in pretty bad shape."

"How bad?"

The nurse didn't answer. Instead she asked in a really gentle voice, "Is there someone here with you?"

I was getting awfully tired of people assuming there was someone here with me. "Just tell me how bad he's hurt, okay? Please?"

I could tell by the sad way she was looking at me that it was pretty bad. "He's got a broken leg, a broken back, and some internal injuries," she said finally. "We still don't know the extent of all his injuries."

I swallowed hard, then stood up a little straighter. I could handle this. "Can I see him?" I asked.

"You can..." She hesitated. "But you have to understand he's pretty banged up. I'm not sure you'll even recognize him—"

"I don't care. I want to see him."

"Okay," the nurse said. "He's under sedation, but you can see him for a little bit if you want to. No more than ten minutes, though, okay?"

I nodded.

The nurse led the way through the double doors, and I followed her into a huge, brightly lit open area with a desk in the middle and little glass rooms on all the sides. A telephone rang. The nurse turned toward the sound, frowned, then turned back to me. "I'm sorry, but I have to get that," she said. She pointed toward a darkened room across the way. "Your dad's over there."

"Okay. Thank you," I said. But she was already gone.

I took a deep breath, then forced my legs to carry me the

rest of the way to Joe's room. I stopped just outside the door and slowly poked my head around the corner. All I could see was a white blanket that covered his legs and feet. One of his legs was a lot bigger around than the other one, like there was a cast or something on it, but I couldn't actually see the cast through the blanket.

I took another breath, then stepped into the room. I edged closer to the bed. My eyes followed the white blanket from Joe's feet up to his stomach and chest. Several wires ran under the covers to a machine next to the bed. I watched his chest rise and fall a few times before I raised my eyes all the way to his face.

I gasped.

That nurse wasn't kidding about the bruising. A big white bandage circled most of Joe's head, but even in the dark I could see that the skin that was visible between the bandages was a blend of nasty shades of red and purple. Even his eyelids were purple. A fat, bluish tube was taped to his mouth and ran to a machine beside the bed.

I went over and sat down carefully on the bed. I was afraid to move at all because I didn't want to jar him in any way.

This looked bad. *Really* bad.

"Joe?" I said softly, my eyes glued to his face. "Can you hear me, Joe?"

No response.

The only sounds in the room were the hum of the machine with a bunch of lights that stood next to the bed and Joe's steady breathing in and out through that tube. It sounded scary. Like that machine forcing air in and out of Joe's lungs was the only thing keeping him alive.

I shifted on the bed so I could reach under the blanket and hold his hand, but his hands were tied down. His whole body was tied down. Why would they tie him down? I wondered.

I didn't know what to do, so I just sat there and watched him breathe. In and out. In and out.

After a little while, I wiggled myself in between Joe's arm and the bed railing, then slowly leaned over and laid my head down on the pillow next to Joe's shoulder. It smelled like soap and bandages and medicine. I watched his chest rise and fall and listened to his raspy breathing. As I listened, I tried to match his breathing with my own. As though my breathing could somehow make him better. After a little while, my eyelids grew heavy. I pulled my legs up onto the bed and shifted around so I didn't take up much space. I lay on my side, my back resting against the hard metal bar of Joe's bed and my forehead resting against his shoulder. I just needed to rest my eyes for a few minutes...then—

"Hey, you can't sleep here!"

What?

"You can't sleep here," the voice repeated. "You aren't even supposed to be in here for more than ten minutes at a time."

For a second I wasn't even sure where *here* was. Then I smelled those medicine-y bandages, I heard Joe's raspy breathing, and I felt the bar on the hospital bed pressing into my back.

I was at the hospital. With Joe. And I had fallen asleep.

I lifted my head toward the voice and blinked because the light out in that main area was so bright.

"You have to get up. You have to leave," a woman in a nurse's uniform said. But it wasn't the nice nurse from before. This nurse was shorter and skinnier and had a tangle of reddish curls all around her face.

I started to sit up. I squinted at my watch: 12:04 a.m.

I groaned. The last thing I wanted to do was walk all the way home at 12:04 in the morning. I wanted to stay here. With Joe. I was about to ask the nurse if there was someplace else I could go here in the hospital, but a machine out in that main room beeped and the nurse hurried away.

I propped myself up on my elbow and glanced down at Joe. He hadn't moved an inch the entire time I'd been here. If anything, the bruises on his face had gotten worse instead of better. I ached when I looked at him.

I got up off the bed and tiptoed over to the doorway. It looked like the emergency, whatever it was, was in the room directly across from Joe's. That room was all lit up and people in uniforms bustled in and out.

Maybe they were busy enough over there that no one would notice if I stayed with Joe just a little longer. There was a straight chair in the corner of the room and a curtain that hung from the ceiling beside the chair. I didn't dare pull the curtain all the way closed. The nurse would notice that. But maybe I could slide it over a little, just enough to hide behind.

I checked to make sure that nurse wasn't coming back. Then I arranged the curtain and chair so that the only way anyone would know I was still here was if they came all the way in and walked around the bed. I scooted the chair as close to Joe's bed as I dared. Then I sat down and waited to see if I was going to get caught.

I heard someone come in a few minutes later and do something with one of the machines on the other side of Joe's bed. I couldn't see who it was, but I could hear them. I barely breathed. They came back and did the exact same thing about half an hour later. If they came back after that, I never knew it because eventually I fell asleep again.

Chapter Four

A loud clattering jarred me awake. I heard frantic footsteps. And beeping. Something was beeping. What
was going on?

I sat up and peered around the curtain. Joe was still
sound asleep. Whatever was happening, it wasn't happening in here; it was happening in the room across from Joe's
again.

I yawned and stretched my arms out in front of me. I
could tell I'd been sleeping in an awkward position because
my neck hurt. I massaged it with the palm of my hand.
While I was massaging, that crabby redheaded nurse
walked by. She did a double take, then backed up and
poked her head in Joe's room. "Have you been hiding
behind that curtain all night?" she demanded.

"No!" I said. I glanced up at the clock: 5:20. Okay,
maybe I had been here most of the night, but so what? It
wasn't like I was bothering anyone.

The nurse walked all the way into the room and stood
in front of me. I returned her stare.

Her face softened. "You don't have anyone to stay with while your dad's in the hospital, do you?" she asked.

"I do, too."

The nurse just looked at me. She didn't believe me.

"There are all kinds of people I could stay with," I insisted. I started counting them off on my fingers, "Friends. Neighbors. I even have a grandma." Just because Gram was at Valley View didn't mean I didn't have her. "In fact, I live at my grandma's house." This was true.

I stood up and made a big show of looking at the clock. "Wow! My grandma must be worried sick. I better go." I started moving toward the door.

"Why isn't your grandma here at the hospital with you?" the nurse asked, blocking my way.

Why can't you just mind your own business? "Well, she would've been here, but...she's sick. Not just worried sick, but *sick* sick!" Joe always said the best lies had an element of truth to them.

"I should go," I said again. I didn't want to, but if I hung around much longer, this woman was probably going to call Social Services on me.

I went over to the bed so I could whisper in Joe's ear. "I'll be back later, okay?" Just in case he could hear me. Then I made tracks for the elevator.

It was getting light out when I left the hospital. Considering how early it was, there was more traffic on York Avenue than I would've expected. Where were all these people going so early in the morning? I wondered as I walked along the curb.

When I got home, Sherlock was jumping around like crazy. Poor thing. No one had been here to let him out before bed last night. "I'm so sorry, boy," I said, reaching to pick him up. But he slipped out of my hands and made a mad dash for the back door. He *really* had to go.

"Okay, okay," I said, hurrying after him. I opened the back door and out he ran.

While I stood on the back step, watching my dog, I wondered if there was anything I needed to do while Joe was in the hospital. Was everything at the hospital taken care of? Did they know we didn't have money to pay for whatever was wrong with Joe? Was that okay? Was there anyone I needed to call? Probably not Joe's work. His boss was the one who'd called me and told me Joe had been taken to the hospital, so he knew Joe wouldn't be at work today. We didn't really have any other family, except for Gram.

Oh, man. How would I tell Gram what had happened? I had to tell her, didn't I?

I couldn't tell her over the phone; I'd have to go to the nursing home and tell her in person. But what would I say? I didn't even know what all was wrong with Joe. I just knew it was bad. Really bad.

I sighed. Why did this have to happen? Why did it have to happen now? Aside from Gram going into the nursing home, and all that stuff that happened with Suzanne and Sam, things had been going so good for me and Joe. Joe was totally, one hundred percent clean. We were living in an actual house for the first time ever. Okay, it was Gram's house, but at least it wasn't a crappy one-room apartment.

Or a camper. Joe had a job so we could actually afford to buy stuff like food and bus passes and a dog.

Everything was going great until his accident.

Well, at least I wouldn't have to go to Iowa now. That was one good thing about Joe getting hurt. No one would expect me to go away while Joe was in the hospital. Of course the first thing Suzanne would want to know was who was taking care of me. Joe knew I was fine by myself. And I knew I was fine by myself. But Suzanne would probably have a fit if she found out.

I would just have to make sure she never found out.

Woof! Sherlock stood in front of me, wagging his tail. "Are you done?" I asked him.

He let out another woof.

We went inside and I got him some food and fresh water. I grabbed another monster burrito for myself out of the freezer. We only had two more left. But we had peanut butter. And boxes of macaroni and cheese. I'd be okay for a while.

I put my burrito in the microwave, but once it was done I realized I was more tired than hungry. So I took a couple bites of the burrito, then wrapped it up and stuck it back in the fridge. After that I went into my room to try and take a nap. But once I got in bed, I couldn't seem to get comfortable. I kept rolling around and flopping from side to side. Then I felt something kind of bulky poking me in the back. I reached underneath me and pulled out my old stuffed monkey, Chester.

"I have a monkey just like this at home," Sam had said when she saw it three weeks ago.

"You couldn't have one just like it," I'd told her. Chester was a one-of-a-kind monkey. Gram made him for me.

But Sam had insisted she had the same monkey. *"Does Joe ever call himself the Monkey Man?"* she'd asked.

"The Monkey Man?"

"Yeah. You know that song, 'Do You Know the Muffin Man?' Did Joe ever sing it as 'Do You Know the Monkey Man?'"

I had no clue what she was talking about, so she started singing the song. *"Do you know...the monkey man, the monkey man, the monkey man? Do you know...the monkey man, who lives on Drury Lane?"* Then she started on the second verse, *"Yes, I know...the monkey man, the monkey man—"*

I'd stopped her right there. *"Joe? Sing?"* I'd said.

But he used to sing. He used to sing for money. In bars. I remember this guy making me a soft bed of towels under a counter, and I remember drifting off to sleep to the sound of people clapping for my dad.

I didn't remember any Monkey Man song, though. I finally asked Joe, just a couple of days ago, whether he'd ever sung "Do You Know the Monkey Man?" to me.

He smiled. *"You remember that?"*

"Sort of," I lied. I hated that Sam knew something about Joe that I didn't. I was the one who'd lived with him all these years, not her.

"Why did you stop singing?" I asked.

"I had to take care of you," he'd answered.

Oh.

But he never *had* to take care of me. He didn't have to take me away from Suzanne. He chose to do that. But that was because he couldn't bear to lose me. And even though

33

he lied to me all these years, he gave up his whole life…all his dreams, everything, just to take care of me. I needed to remember that.

Well, obviously I wasn't going to fall asleep. I tossed Chester aside, threw off the covers, and went to take a quick shower. If the nurses who worked at the hospital were like the ones who worked at Valley View, they probably changed shifts at seven a.m. Which meant the crabby redheaded nurse would be gone. It was safe to go back.

This time I took the bus. It let me off at the mall across the street from the hospital. I crossed at the crosswalk, went inside, and took the elevator up to ICU. When I got to Joe's room, I saw his eyes were partially open.

"Joe!" I cried, running over to him. "You're awake! When did you wake up? Do the nurses know you're awake?"

But he couldn't answer me because of that fat blue tube in his mouth.

Had he just woken up that very second? Did he know where he was? Did he know what had happened?

"I'm going to go over to the nurse's station to get someone," I said, backing away.

Joe moaned.

"What?" I asked. "Do they know you're awake?"

He nodded once. It looked like it hurt a lot to do that.

"Oh. Okay." I walked slowly back to the bed. "How are you feeling?" I asked. Which was probably a really stupid question.

Joe sort of grimaced. His face was still all red and swollen between the bandages. If anything, it was even more red and swollen than before.

"Not so good, huh?"

His eyes were so droopy it looked like he was going to fall back asleep any second. He pantomimed holding a piece of paper in one hand and writing something with the other hand. A giant clothespin-like thing covered his left finger. But hey, at least his hands weren't tied down anymore.

"You want to write something?" I asked.

He nodded. Then he cocked his elbow toward a table on the other side of his bed. There was a white board and a black marker over there. I got them and handed them to Joe.

It was hard for him to write with that thing on his finger. His letters ran uphill across the board and each one was smaller than the one before it. BRKE BAK.

Was that supposed to say "broke back?" As in "I broke my back?"

"I know," I said.

He kept writing. LONG TIM TIL BETER. I had to follow each letter as he wrote it because he wrote right over the top of the words he wrote before.

I swallowed. "I know. But I'll help you get better. I'll take care of you when you come home."

DONT TLL GRM, he wrote.

"What?" I looked up from his message. "Joe, I can't keep something like this from Gram." It was bad enough he didn't want me to tell her about Suzanne and Sam. I had to tell her Joe was in the hospital.

He closed his eyes and let the board fall to the bed.

"No! You can't go to sleep yet. We have to talk about

this. What am I supposed to tell Gram when she asks why you stopped visiting her?"

No response.

"I know you don't want her to freak out. But she's going to freak out anyway," I said.

Joe's eyes remained closed.

"She's not as mixed up as you think she is. Plus she's your mom. Don't you think she should know what happened to you?"

Still nothing.

I sighed. "Fine. If you don't want me to tell Gram you're in the hospital, what *do* you want me to tell her?"

I didn't actually expect an answer. I thought he'd gone back to sleep. But he picked up the white board and I saw his fingers feeling around for pen. I picked it up and put it in his hand.

He opened one eye and scrawled: ANTHG BT TRTH.

Anything but the truth? What? Was that his new motto?

* * *

It looked like Joe was going to sleep for a while, so I decided to head over to the nursing home and visit Gram. It took two buses to get there from the hospital. And then I still had to walk six blocks.

Valley View was a one-story brick building with three separate wings: one for the people who didn't need much extra help, one for the people who needed lots of help, and one for the Alzheimer's patients. Gram had had a stroke; that was why she was at Valley View. Joe thought it was too hard for us to take care of her, which made me mad because I didn't think it was that hard. Then the nurses thought she was also showing signs of Alzheimer's, so they put her in the Alzheimer's wing. That *really* made me mad because Gram was not as crazy as some of those people, and I was afraid that being around crazy people all the time would push Gram over the edge. But I'm a kid, so nobody cared what I thought.

They kept the Alzheimer's wing locked so the patients wouldn't wander out. I punched in the code, and when the door unlocked, I went inside. Yuck. It always smelled like disinfectant and gross food in here.

Gram was stretched out on her bed, sound asleep, when I got to her room. Her mouth hung open at a weird angle and she was snoring.

I eased myself into the rocking chair across from her bed and rocked slowly back and forth while I waited for her to wake up. Her room was about the size of our bathroom, which meant it wasn't very big. The bed took up most of one wall. A bulletin board with old Get Well Soon cards hung above it. The only other thing in the room was the little bureau with the TV on it that stood next to my chair.

That TV used to be in our kitchen. When we first moved in with Gram, I'd sit at the kitchen table with her and we'd watch *Wheel of Fortune* after dinner. She used to be good at it, too. I'd seen her solve puzzles that only had two letters in place. But she couldn't do that anymore.

I reached into my pocket and pulled out a square of bubble gum.

"T.J.," Gram said suddenly.

I jumped. "Gram! Hi," I said, stuffing the gum back inside my pocket. Gram didn't like it when I chewed gum. She said the sugar would rot my teeth.

"How long have you been sitting there?" She squinted at me and tried to sit up. "Where's your dad? He hasn't been to see me all week."

"Joe was here yesterday, Gram," I said. I went over and helped her sit up. "Yesterday morning."

"He was?" Gram looked confused.

"Yes." I sat down next to her on the bed. I felt like I was the grandma and she was the little girl as I reached for her bony hand. "But…he's not going to be able to come back for a while. He's…really, really busy at work."

"What's he doing?" she asked.

"He's…um…working for that builder out in Excelsior, remember? That guy's building like thirty houses right now, so Joe's…well, doing whatever he does at work. He'll be there from seven in the morning until ten at night for the next couple of weeks." Man, I hated lying to her.

"Well, I hope he doesn't work too hard," Gram said.

I helped her into her wheelchair and wheeled her around the nursing home for a while. I wished I could talk to her the way I used to. I wanted to tell her where Joe really was. I wanted to tell her I was scared and I didn't know if I had done everything I needed to do. I also wanted to tell her about Sam and Suzanne, and I wanted to ask her why she never told me the truth about who I was. I'd wanted to ask her that every time I'd seen her over the last three weeks. But I wasn't supposed to bring up any of that.

"I should go," I told Gram. It was time for her afternoon snack in the big activities room down the hall, and I'd already been away from the hospital longer than I'd wanted to be.

"Okay," Gram said. "Tell your dad to come and see me. I haven't seen him all week."

I sighed. She'd forgotten everything I said already. "Okay, Gram," I said, bending to kiss her cheek. "I'll tell him."

The buses didn't line up very well for my trip back to the hospital. I had to wait half an hour for the second bus. But eventually it came and I hopped on and took a seat at the front. I thought about getting off at my street so I could go let Sherlock out again before I headed back to the hospital, but it hadn't been that long since I let him out. He should be okay. I stayed on the bus all the way to the mall, then got out and walked across to the hospital.

I hurried inside and took the elevator up to the third floor. But when I got to Joe's little glass room, his bed was empty.

It was all made up as though he'd never been there.

Chapter Five

I strode over to the two new nurses who were sitting at the big desk in the main room. "Where's my dad?" I demanded.

"Who is your dad?" the one with the glasses and bad dye job asked.

"Joseph Wright. He was in that room over there." I pointed, panic rising in my chest.

The dark-haired nurse slid some papers around on her desk. "He was moved," she said finally.

Oh, thank God! I'd been afraid—well, never mind what I'd been afraid of. "Moved where?"

"To a regular room."

A regular room? That was good, right? "Then he must be doing better."

"He's stable. I'll get you the room number." She flipped through a few more papers. "Here it is. Room 515. Go out those doors and—"

"I'll find it," I said, hurrying away. I took the elevator up two floors, then followed the signs to room 515.

Joe was in the bed over by the window. The big tube in his mouth was gone now, but he had a skinny clear tube running into each nostril. He didn't see me because he was looking out the window.

"Looks like you're doing better," I said, marching into the room. Oh. He had a roommate now. Some skinny old guy who hardly had any hair and whistled when he snored.

Joe turned his head slowly toward me. He didn't look much better. He was still all bruised and swollen. His eyes sort of sank into his head. But at least he could talk to me now that he didn't have that tube in his mouth.

"How are you feeling?" I asked, lowering my voice so I wouldn't wake the roommate up.

"Throat's sore." Joe rubbed his throat. "From the tube." It sounded sore, too, the way he was talking.

"Yeah, but the rest of you is getting better, right? Otherwise they wouldn't have moved you to a regular room."

He didn't respond to that. "Have…you…seen Gram?" he asked. I had to listen really hard to make out what he was saying.

"Yes." I grabbed a chair and dragged it closer to the bed. "I was just there. She's okay. She's having a regular day. Not good or bad. Just regular."

"Did you…tell her…about me?"

"No!" I couldn't believe he even asked. "You told me not to."

"Doesn't…mean…you…didn't."

"I didn't," I said. Jeez! "I told her you were busy at work and you wouldn't be able to visit for a while. But she forgot ten minutes later."

"What about…your mother?" It was such an effort for him to talk.

My mother? "You mean Suzanne? What about her?"

"Have…you…called…her?"

I assumed he meant have you called her *to tell her you're not coming?* "Not yet," I said. "I don't know what to say. I don't want to tell her you're in the hospital. She'll want to know who's staying with me—"

"You…should still go…to Iowa."

"What?" I cried. "No!"

"Yes."

"You're in the hospital. I'm not going to Iowa while you're in the hospital." What kind of person goes off on a big trip when her dad is in the hospital?

Joe shifted position and winced. "The hospital social worker…came around…asked questions…about you. Lots of questions. You can't…stay alone…at the house. I said…you were staying…with a neighbor."

"Good," I said. Except I'd told that nurse this morning that I was staying with my grandma. I hoped the nurse and the social worker didn't talk to each other.

"I also said…you're going…to your mom's…tomorrow. You should go…like we planned."

"No," I said. "I don't want to. I don't want to leave you."

"Yes," he insisted. He closed his eyes. "Otherwise Suzanne…will think…something's wrong." His breathing grew slow and heavy, like he was asleep. I sat and watched him for about fifteen minutes. Then I got up and went home.

* * *

There was no way I was going to Iowa, I thought as I sat cross-legged on the recliner in front of the TV, eating my Kraft macaroni and cheese right out of the pan. Absolutely no way. And I would call Suzanne and tell her so as soon as I finished eating. I'd tell her somebody really important to me was in the hospital and I couldn't possibly go to Iowa right now. Of course, she'll want to know who's in the hospital, so I'll tell her my best friend was in a terrible accident. Hmmm...I'll need a name for that friend...

The doorbell rang. Sherlock's ears perked up and he let out a short woof as he got up and trotted down the hall. I followed him, carrying the pot of macaroni and cheese with me.

Great. It was my social worker, Mrs. Morris.

Sherlock stood at the door and barked at her, but he didn't scare her away. "May I come in, T.J.?" she asked, her hand already on the outside door handle.

"I guess." She was already most of the way in anyway.

Mrs. Morris was an older lady with a long black and gray braid that she wore twisted around her head. Even though it was summer, she always came to our house dressed in a nice skirt and matching jacket. She peered inside my pot and wrinkled her nose. Then I saw her glance with disapproval at the basket of dirty laundry sitting in the middle of our living room. What? Didn't she ever have dirty laundry?

"I heard about your dad," she said, her eyes returning to my face. "I'm sorry."

"Thanks," I said. "But he's not dead. He's just hurt. He'll be okay. How did you know he was in the hospital anyway?"

"Our office received a call from the hospital social worker. They said they had a patient who possibly had a child home alone. When I heard the name of the patient, I put two and two together."

"Oh, I'm not staying here alone," I assured Mrs. Morris.

"Really," Mrs. Morris said, looking around. "Who's staying here with you?"

I gulped. "Well, no one's actually staying *here*," I admitted. "I'm staying next door." Hadn't Joe said he told the hospital social worker that I was staying with a neighbor?

Mrs. Morris pressed her lips together. "Then why are you here now, eating dinner all by yourself?"

She thought she had me, but she didn't. "I came home to do laundry," I said, gesturing toward the big basket. "And to get packed for my trip. I'm supposed to go visit Suzanne tomorrow, remember?"

I'm so smart I amaze myself sometimes.

"Yes. That's the other reason I'm here," Mrs. Morris said. "I wanted to see if your plans had changed now that your dad is in the hospital."

I couldn't tell whether she thought my plans *should* have changed or not. "No, he's doing pretty good," I lied. "And he said I should still go." That part was true.

"Well. Your mother will be happy to hear that."

"Did you tell her Joe was in the hospital?" I asked, feeling a little panicked.

"No." Mrs. Morris looked surprised. "I thought you would have called her."

Whew. What a relief. "I haven't had time," I said. "I'll call her as soon as I finish my supper." *To let her know I'm not coming.*

I edged closer toward the door, hoping Mrs. Morris would get the hint. She did, but when she got to the door, she stopped. "So, which neighbor are you staying with?" she asked.

"The one over there." I pointed loosely toward Dave and Nick's house.

Mrs. Morris slipped out the door, took a closer look at the house I just pointed at, then started across the grass in her high heels.

I poked my head out the door. "What are you doing?" I asked.

"I want to check in with your neighbor."

Uh-oh. Dave and Nick's parents were nice, but they wouldn't tell Mrs. Morris I was staying there when I wasn't.

I went all the way outside. "I don't think they're home," I called. But Mrs. Morris kept right on walking.

I watched nervously as she marched up the brick steps and rang the bell. When no one came to the door, she rang the bell again. For once, luck was on my side. They really weren't home!

"Told you," I said as she made her way back to my house.

Mrs. Morris glanced over at their house once more, then pressed her lips together. I could tell she was trying to decide what to do. "You're sure you're staying over there tonight?" she asked. "You're not staying here by yourself?"

"Of course not." I loved how she actually expected me to tell her I was lying.

"And you're really going to your mom's tomorrow?"

"Yes."

Mrs. Morris still didn't look entirely convinced. "Okay," she said finally. Then she got in her car and drove away.

But all of a sudden I realized people were going to be checking on me if I stayed here by myself. That one nurse at the hospital had already been suspicious enough about me to call Social Services. She'd call again if they saw me hanging around. Which meant it was going to be hard to visit Joe. In fact, Mrs. Morris might actually call Suzanne to make sure I really did show up. If Suzanne found out that 1) I'd lied to her, 2) Joe was in the hospital, and 3) no one was staying with me, she wouldn't just make me come and stay with her for a week, she'd make me stay there for good.

Joe wasn't dying or anything. In fact, he was getting better. He was out of the ICU. He could talk. And…he'd told me to go to Iowa.

Maybe I should go?

But what about Gram? Could I really go away when I knew Joe wouldn't be able to visit Gram? She probably wouldn't have any visitors the whole time I was gone.

Did I have a choice? It was better to go to Iowa now and

be able to come back than to not go and get taken away from Joe forever.

So I spent the rest of the evening cramming all the stuff I thought I'd need for the next week into Joe's old duffel bag. Pair of jeans, couple of pairs of shorts, T-shirts, socks, underwear. Of course, I was going to a wedding, so I needed something dressy, too. I didn't have a lot of fancy clothes. Just a pair of black pants and a white shirt that Gram bought me for my band concert last winter. I hoped they still fit. I grabbed the pants and shirt off their hangers, folded them neatly and laid them on top of all my other stuff in the duffel. I went into the bathroom to get my toothbrush, toothpaste, and shampoo, shoved them into the side pocket, then zipped the duffel closed.

"I guess that's it," I told Sherlock. I sank to the floor beside him and he climbed into my lap. I buried my face in his fur and hugged him hard. "What if Joe gets worse while I'm gone, Sherlock?" I asked.

I'd have to call Joe while I was in Iowa. I didn't have a cell phone and I didn't know if Suzanne would let me use her phone to call him, but I would find a way to talk to him. I'd seen a phone in his room, but I didn't know the number. I would have to go to the hospital one more time to say good-bye to Joe before I went to Iowa anyway. I could see if the number was written on the phone while I was there.

"Is there anything else I need to do before I go?" I asked my dog.

"Oh, my gosh! *Sherlock!*" I cried. What was I going to do with him while I was gone? Joe couldn't take care of him.

The only people I knew well enough to ask were Dave and Nick next door. But I didn't really want to ask them. They had a dog get run over by a car once. Plus they weren't even home.

Would it be crazy to take him to Iowa with me?

I called the bus station to see whether they allowed dogs on the bus. They did. I thought about calling Suzanne, too, to make sure it was okay with her if I brought Sherlock. But what if she said no? It was better to just show up with him. Then she wouldn't be able to say no.

I filled an old ice cream bucket with dog food and set it in a big grocery bag along with Sherlock's bowls, his leash, and a couple of toys. I put that bag next to my duffel. Now I really was ready.

I set my alarm for five o'clock in the morning so I'd have time to go see Joe before I left for the bus station. Then I went to bed.

But once again, I couldn't sleep. My brain just wouldn't shut off. I worried about Joe, and I worried about Gram. I even worried about Suzanne and Sam. What would they be like? I wondered. Would they expect me to just blend right into their family while I was there? Would I be able to keep the fact that Joe was in the hospital a secret?

At a quarter to five, I gave up on sleep. I got up, took a quick shower, then jogged over to the hospital. I ran along the sidewalk, cut through the mall parking lot, and arrived at the hospital at exactly five thirty.

I wasn't sure I was actually allowed to visit Joe this early, but there wasn't anyone sitting at the main desk to stop me, so I zipped across the lobby and ducked into a waiting elevator. When I got to the fifth floor I saw a couple of nurses talking quietly at the other end of the hall, but they didn't pay any attention to me. I kept on going, all the way to Joe's room.

I wasn't surprised to find the room dark and both Joe and his roommate sound asleep. The roommate was whistling again. I tiptoed over to the phone. There was enough light from the hallway that I could read the number on it. I found a pen in a drawer, but no paper. So I picked up the pen and copied the number onto the palm of my hand. Then I went over to Joe.

At first I just watched him sleep. I watched him inhale and exhale loudly through his open mouth. He sure wasn't going to wake up on his own, so I leaned over him and whispered, "Joe? Joe, it's me. Wake up."

His eyelids fluttered open and he blinked a couple of times in my direction. "T.J.?"

"I-I'm going to Iowa," I said.

"Okay," he said drowsily. He closed his eyes.

"You said you wanted me to go," I reminded him. But I could still change my mind. All he had to do was say, "Don't go, T.J.," and I wouldn't.

"Behave yourself while you're there," he said, his eyes still closed. "Make them think I raised you right." And then he was asleep again.

My eyes welled with tears, but I blinked them away. I leaned down and kissed his forehead. "I'll be back in a week," I whispered.

Chapter Six

How was I supposed to get to the bus station with my duffel, my dog, and all my dog's stuff? It was too far to walk. I couldn't take a city bus. Not with Sherlock. About the only other thing I could think of to do was call a cab, so that was what I did. I had to use some of the money Suzanne sent me for the bus to pay for it, which meant that when I got to the bus station, I didn't have enough left for a round-trip ticket to Cedar Rapids, Iowa. I only had enough for a one-way ticket.

If I couldn't afford a round-trip ticket, how would I get home next week? Well, I'd worry about that next week. Right now, I had to get to Iowa. "One way to Cedar Rapids, Iowa," I told the guy at the ticket counter. His name tag said "Tony."

The bus was already boarding, so as soon as I got my ticket, I threw my duffel bag onto my shoulder, grabbed Sherlock's leash in one hand and his bag of stuff in the other, then hustled toward the double doors.

"Excuse me, miss," Tony called after me.

I turned.

"You can't take your dog on the bus like that."

"Are you kidding me?" I stomped back over to the counter. "I called here last night. Whoever I talked to said dogs were allowed."

"They are. In the cargo bay. Do you have a kennel or something to transport him in?"

"No," I said. We never bought a kennel because Sherlock always slept on my bed. "He's small, though. I can keep him on my lap the whole time."

Tony shook his head. "I'm sorry. Pets have to ride in the cargo bay."

I sighed. What was I supposed to do? I was already here. With my dog. I had a ticket for the bus, but no kennel. I didn't even have enough money to take a cab back home if this guy wasn't going to let Sherlock on the bus.

"We might have a spare kennel in the back room," Tony said. "Let me go check." He went away for a couple of minutes, then came back with a huge, way-too-big-for-Sherlock kennel that smelled like dirty dogs.

Was he serious? He wanted me to put my dog in that? Who knew what diseases were lurking inside there?

"I'll carry it out to the bus for you," Tony said, lifting it up over the counter as he bumped the little gate open with his hip.

"Gee, thanks," I muttered. I followed him out to the bus. The gas fumes and cigarette smoke made me feel a little sick to my stomach. Tony set the kennel down in front of the open cargo bay, and a guy in a bus driver uniform came over to check it out.

"Looks like we've got some special cargo for this trip," the bus driver said, bending down to scratch Sherlock behind the ears.

"Yup," I said. I waited until Tony left, then asked, "Do I really have to put my dog in there? Couldn't I just hold him on my lap?" The bus driver seemed nice. And he obviously liked dogs.

"Sorry." He shook his head. "It's against the rules."

Personally, I always thought rules were made to be broken. Especially when they were stupid rules to begin with. But the bus driver made it clear that the only way my dog was getting on this bus was in a kennel. In the cargo bay.

"Sorry, boy," I said, dropping to my knees. I hugged my dog hard, then I pointed toward the open kennel. "I guess you have to go in there."

His tail drooped. He just looked at me and whined.

"I know," I said, giving his back end a nudge. "I wouldn't want to do it, either. And I wouldn't make you if I didn't have to." I pushed him all the way in. The bus driver closed the door behind him, picked up the kennel like it was just a light briefcase, and set it in the cargo bay.

Sherlock pawed at the door and whined some more, which about broke my heart. He would probably whine the whole way to Iowa. I hoped the bus driver was happy.

I felt all choky inside as I climbed onto the bus. An old lady who was knitting in the front seat smiled at me, but I kept moving. At least there were lots of open seats. I chose one in the middle, tossed my duffel bag onto the window seat, and plopped into the aisle seat so no one would sit down with me. Then I reclined my seat back as far as it would go and settled in for the long ride.

Once we got out of the Twin Cities, there wasn't much to see. Just one field of corn after another, broken up by the occasional bean field. I wondered how Sherlock was doing in the cargo bay. It was probably dark under there. Was he scared? Was he bus sick? Or had he simply curled up and gone to sleep?

I wanted to sleep, but I couldn't. I was too worried about Sherlock...and Joe...and Gram...and this whole upcoming week. As I rested my head against the window I thought back to that day that changed everything. The day I met Sam.

I first noticed her in the park when I was on my way home from softball. It was her hair that caught my attention; it was the exact same color as mine and Joe's. You don't see people with hair as light as ours very often. She was with another girl, a girl with darker hair, and they were sitting on the merry-go-round, in the boiling hot sun, talking. I didn't know why anyone would want to sit out in the sun on such a hot day, but I was too hot and sweaty myself to care what anyone else was doing. I just wanted to get home.

But then she'd called out to me. "Tara?"

Tara? Everyone always called me T.J.

I turned around and even from a distance I could tell we kind of looked alike.

"Oh, my God!" she said, running up to me. "You really are alive."

What?

"Your name's Sarah, right?" she said when I didn't say anything. *Sarah,* not Tara.

"My name's T.J.," I said. Then I turned and walked away. But she and that other girl followed me. I could hear them talking behind me. Sam thought I was her sister; the friend said she was wrong; they started arguing.

I crossed the street and was about to go in my house when one of them yelled, "WAIT!"

Sam came barreling across the street. "You live *here?*" She was out of breath from running so fast. "Is Joseph Wright your dad?"

She was exactly my height. Her hair was way longer than mine, but both her hair and her eyes were the same color as mine. And there was something about her face... She wore quite a bit of makeup, which was all blotchy because of the heat, but underneath the makeup, her face looked strangely like mine.

My head warned: *Get away...go inside...don't talk to this girl.* But my feet refused to budge. "Who are you?" I asked. How did she know my dad?

"I'm Sam!" she said as though that explained everything.

I didn't know any Sam.

I used to have a brother named Sam. He died in a fire with my parents when I was three. I hardly remembered him. What were the odds that this girl who thought I was her sister, this girl who kind of looked like me, would have the same name as my dead brother?

"Don't you know who I am?" She really, really wanted me to know who she was, but I had no idea.

"I'm Samantha Wright. Joseph Wright is my dad."

Joe had a kid?

That was impossible. Joe wasn't even my real dad. He was my dad's friend. He took me in when my whole family died and he adopted me...because he and my real dad were friends. That was what he'd always told me.

I tried to tell her she was confused, but she shook her head. "No. Joseph Wright is your real dad. He's my dad, too. And you're my sister. My twin sister. Your dad used to be married to my mom and we all lived together in Clearwater, Iowa. But then you drowned in the quarry when we were three. At least, that's what everyone thought. And after that our parents got divorced and my dad went away and I haven't seen him since."

She told me she wanted to find her dad, so she went to a psychic. The psychic couldn't help her, but she told Sam that her sister was still alive. Sam didn't believe it at first, but then she found all these newspaper articles in her basement that talked about how three-year-old Sarah Wright was out in a canoe with her dad, Joseph, and the canoe capsized. Sarah drowned. But her body was never found.

Sam thought *I* was Sarah.

This had to be a joke. A really bad one. Except...*Joe had said I was born in a town called Clearwater, Iowa.* I didn't remember it; I was a baby when I lived there, and I'd never been back. But that was the name of the town where I'd been born. How did she know?

As Sam kept talking, I saw a picture of a pink bathroom in my head. It had a pink toilet and pink carpet and there was a picture of a ballerina on the wall. I was in the tub, splashing around with my...*brother*, right? It had to be my brother because I only ever had a brother. I never had any sisters.

But this was a brand new memory. And I was pretty sure the other kid in the tub was a girl.

No. It couldn't be.

Sam blabbered on about how she hired some detective over the Internet to find her dad, and how she did this all behind her mom's back because her mom never talked about Joe and didn't believe I could still be alive. The detective gave her phone numbers for three different Joseph Wrights and she called them all. That was how she knew she had the right Joseph.

"You mean you actually talked to Joe?" I asked.

"Well, no," she admitted. "I heard his voice on the answering machine. I left a message, but he never called me back."

I didn't remember any strange message on our machine, but she swore she left one. And she was one hundred percent positive she had the right Joseph Wright. She said she called again when Joe didn't call her back, but our phone was disconnected. She said it like that proved Joe was her dad.

What? Did she think Joe heard her message and then had our phone disconnected to get rid of her? It's true, our phone was disconnected for a while, but that was because we hadn't paid the bill, not because Joe and me were on the

56

run. If we were on the run, wouldn't we have just run again when Sam called rather than disconnect our phone?

Maybe not, a small voice inside me said. *Not when we were living in Gram's house and Gram was in a nursing home.*

"We could probably clear this whole thing up really fast if you have a picture of your dad," Sam's friend said. "Something so Sam can see whether or not she's got the right Joseph Wright."

We didn't have a lot of pictures. Joe wasn't real big on taking pictures. But I let Sam and her friend come into our house to see what we had. I thought it was the quickest way to get rid of them. We had a photo album on the shelf in the closet; I went to get it. The earliest picture we had of me was my kindergarten school picture. Joe always said my baby pictures got burned in the fire. I flipped through until I found a picture of Joe. It was one I took of him in our backyard when I needed a picture of my family for school.

"That's him!" Sam cried. "I know it's him!"

How did she know? I wondered. She just said she hadn't seen him since she was three years old.

She had a picture she wanted me to look at, too. It wasn't a picture of Joe. It was a picture of two little blond girls who were dressed in matching pink dresses and standing in front of a white house.

"Is one of those girls you?" Sam asked.

I shivered. It was ninety-eight degrees outside and I was shivering. "I don't know," I said. But I couldn't help but notice that the girl on the right had a mole on the left side of her chin. Just like mine.

I called Joe and left a message for him to come home. While we waited, Sam asked me a bunch of questions. We found out we had some weird things in common. Like our birthdays. We had the same birthday, except she was a year older than me. *If we really were twins, how could she be a year older than me?* We both named our pets Sherlock, but she had a cat and I had a dog. And then there was the whole thing with Chester. *How could she possibly have a monkey just like the one Gram made especially for me?*

When Joe got home, he didn't have to say a word. I could tell by the way he looked at Sam that every single thing she said was true.

I couldn't deal with this. I couldn't deal with any of it, so I ran next door, hoping to hide out in Nick and David's house. But Joe came to get me right away. We sat outside our house and he tried to explain, but there was no explaining it. My dad—and he admitted he really was my dad—had told everyone I was dead and then he had taken me away.

Joe told me we'd moved around a lot those first few years. He had worked when he could, but mostly we'd lived on money Gram sent us. Joe had changed my name, my age, our whole family history. I could hardly wrap my brain around everything I was hearing. I just kept thinking, *you lied to me. You lied to me about everything.*

We were still sitting there when three police cars pulled up in front of our house. While Joe and I were talking, Sam was inside our house calling her mom. After they hung up, her mom had called the police. Everything happened really fast after that.

We all rode to the police station in separate cars: Joe, Sam, and me. A lady police officer who said her name was Officer Kroll took me into a room that reminded me of the counselor's office at school. She asked me to tell her what had just happened, but I couldn't. One minute I was on my way home from softball, the next minute my entire life had been turned upside down.

Some time later Suzanne showed up at the police station.

"Oh, my God," she said when she saw me for the first time.

I have to admit that those exact same words went through my head when I looked at her. *This was my mother. I actually had a mother.*

No. I didn't want to believe it. And it was pretty easy to tell myself she wasn't my mother because we didn't look anything alike. Her hair was darker than mine and Sam's, and her face was rounder. But then she ran over and threw her arms around me, hugging me so hard she squeezed the air right out of me. Her tears dribbled all over my shoulder and all I could do was stand there. I don't think I even hugged her back.

"When can I take her home?" Suzanne asked the two police officers who were standing in the doorway.

"What?" I backed away. "No!" I shouted. "I'm not going with her." Where did she think she was going to take me, anyway? To *Iowa?* No way!

I was pretty mad at Joe, but I never once thought I wouldn't stay with him.

"How do we know she is who she says she is?" I asked Officer Kroll. "Does anyone have any DNA proof that she's really my…" I couldn't even say the word. To say it out loud was to admit it. *She was my mother.*

"Of course I'm your mother," Suzanne said, her eyes filling with fresh tears. "You can tell just by looking at us that I'm her mother, can't you?" she asked the three police officers. "Can't you?" The tears spilled down her cheeks.

I didn't care who she was. "I'm not going with her," I said again. She couldn't make me. "I want to go home. I want to see Joe."

Suzanne's eyes flashed and for a second I thought she was going to hit me. But instead she got right in my face and said, "You are never going to see Joseph Wright again!"

Well, I wasn't going to let her tell me who I could and could not see. I started yelling at her and she started yelling at me and eventually the police had to separate us. They took Suzanne away and that was the last I saw of her. I met Mrs. Morris right after that and she took me to a foster home that night, which was kind of scary. I shared an attic room with four other girls, one of whom cried half the night. I didn't cry, though. I never cried. I just lay awake and wondered what was going to happen to me.

The next morning Mrs. Morris picked me up and took me to see a judge. The guy didn't look or act much like a judge. He wore jeans and a T-shirt and instead of sitting behind a big desk in a courtroom, he took me to a cafeteria in the basement of the courthouse. He bought me a muffin and a carton of orange juice. Then we sat down at a table and talked.

He wanted to know what living with Joe had been like the last ten years. Where had we lived? Not just what city, but what kind of house or apartment? What kind of jobs did Joe have? Was he home when I was or did he leave me home alone? Did I get clothes and shoes when I needed them? Did I go to the doctor and the dentist? Did I have enough to eat? Did he ever do anything illegal?

I told the judge Joe was great, which he was. Mostly. *When he wasn't lying to me.*

Then the judge wanted to know what I thought about Suzanne.

I shrugged. "I don't know her."

"Would you like to know her?"

That seemed like a trick question. There was no right answer. If I said yes, the judge would make it happen. He'd take me away from Joe and make me go live with her. But if I said no, he'd think Joe had poisoned me against her, and then he'd still take me away from Joe and make me go live with her.

"If it was up to you, T.J.," the judge rephrased his question. "Who do you think I should award custody to?"

"Joe," I said right away. "But that's not going to happen, is it?"

"It could," the judge said, wadding up the paper from his muffin and tossing it on the tray. "Your mother has decided not to fight for custody."

"What?" That was about the last thing I expected him to say.

"You've been with your dad the last ten years," the judge said. "You seem happy and settled with him. Your mother has decided that if you really want to stay with him, you can. As long as we can be certain he really is a good father."

I opened my mouth, but no words came out. I should have been happy. No, I should've been ecstatic. Suzanne wasn't going to make me go live with her. But instead I was just more confused. Yesterday she'd said I would never see Joe again. Now she was going to let me stay with him? Why did she change her mind?

"Of course, your mom would like an opportunity to get to know you. She wants you to come for regular visits, starting…" He riffled through some papers on the table until he found the one he wanted. Then he read from it. "Starting three weeks from right now. She's getting married the first weekend in August and she'd like you to be there for the wedding." He looked up at me. "Would you be willing to do that?"

I shrugged. "I guess." And that was the end of that.

I hadn't seen Suzanne since. She didn't even try and call me once she got back home. Sam called, though. She called a lot. But I never picked up. I didn't know what to say to her.

Then Suzanne wrote me a letter. It began, *My darling daughter.* Not *Dear T.J.* Or worse, *Dear Sarah.* I only read the letter once or twice, but I had the whole thing memorized.

My darling daughter,

> *I know this must be difficult for you. It's difficult*
> *for me, too. But despite everything that's happened,*
> *I can't tell you how happy I am to know that you are alive*
> *and well. I'm so looking forward to getting to know you*

and having you come for monthly visits. I hope you're looking forward to it, too. Please use the enclosed $200 for your bus ticket. I love you more than words can say.

Mom

She didn't even know me. How could she possibly love me?

I never wrote back.

Chapter Seven

I pressed my forehead against the window as we pulled into the bus station parking lot. There weren't a lot of people here, so I saw Suzanne and Sam right away. They were standing in the outside bus lane. It looked like they had dressed up to come and get me. Suzanne was wearing a flowery blue skirt with a white blouse, and Sam was wearing a brand new pair of jeans and a green blouse with poufy sleeves. I just had on an old pair of denim cut-offs with a plain white T-shirt.

They moved closer to the bus and I could tell they were looking for me in all the windows. I leaned back against my seat so they wouldn't see me. I didn't want them to think I was staring at them.

Oh man. I wasn't ready for this. My hands were clammy and I felt really sick to my stomach. I wondered what would happen if I just stayed on the bus and continued on to St. Louis or wherever else this bus was headed? Suzanne would call Mrs. Morris and ask where I was, that's what would happen. Mrs. Morris would call the bus station and they'd track me down. No, staying on the bus was not an option.

I grabbed my duffel bag and followed the other people off the bus.

Sam waved eagerly at me as soon as I stepped onto the curb. She was a lot more excited to see me than I was to see her. But I didn't want her to think I was scared or nervous or anything, so even though my heart was pounding, I took a deep breath and marched over to her.

"Hey," I said, like I was the coolest, most confident person in the world.

"Hey," she said back.

Wow. Take away her long hair and makeup, we really did look alike. Same eyes. Same mouth. Even the same mole on our chins, except hers was on the right and mine was on the left.

"T.J.," Suzanne said, throwing her arms around me and practically knocking me over. "We're so glad you're here!"

I couldn't quite bring myself to hug her back. And I tried not to notice the tears in her eyes when she finally let me go.

"Is that all you brought?" Sam asked, nodding at my duffel.

"No. I'll go get...my other stuff." I headed over to the open cargo bay. The bus driver had already set a bunch of suitcases on the sidewalk and was reaching for Sherlock's kennel. My dog looked a little nervous as his kennel rocked back and forth in the air. Then he saw me and he let out an excited little yip.

"Hey, boy!" I grinned as the bus driver set the kennel down at my feet. "That bag over there is mine, too." I pointed to the grocery bag with Sherlock's stuff, and the bus driver handed it to me.

I could feel Suzanne and Sam moving in closer behind me. I grabbed the leash out of the bag, opened the kennel door, and snapped the leash onto Sherlock's collar. He jumped all over me and started licking my face. "Good boy," I whispered, gently pushing him away. Then I stood up and slowly turned around.

"I-I hope you don't mind that I brought my dog," I said, holding tight to his leash. My heart was pounding a mile a minute.

"Sit," I hissed as my dog yipped and leaped against my leg. But he was too wound up to do what I said. Plus he'd been sitting, or lying down, for the last nine hours.

Suzanne and Sam both had sort of stunned looks on their faces. Suzanne pulled herself together first. "No, of course we don't mind," she said with a forced smile. "Sam, why don't you grab that bag. Do you have any other suitcases, T.J.? Maybe a garment bag?"

Garment bag? What the heck was a garment bag?

"No, this is it." I hoisted my duffel back up onto my shoulder and twisted the leash around my wrist a few times. "And I can carry my own bag." I tried to take it from Sam, but she shifted it to her other arm.

"I've got it," she said.

I heard a jingly tune coming from Sam's purse. Still holding my bag with one arm, she reached into her purse and pulled out a cell phone. It was pink with butterflies on it. "Hello?" she said.

"The car's over there," Suzanne said as she led the way to a dark blue Honda Civic that was parked at a meter in the next block.

Whoever Sam was talking to must've been doing all the talking. All Sam said was, "Yeah...Yeah...Yeah...I don't know...Okay, bye."

Suzanne popped the trunk and we put my duffel and my grocery bag inside.

"Um, Sherlock probably has to go to the bathroom," I said, looking around for some grass I could take him to.

"There's a bike trail back behind those buildings," Sam said as she dropped her phone back into her purse. We walked around the corner and followed a driveway back to a grassy area that led downhill to the river.

"So, how have you been, T.J.?" Suzanne asked when Sherlock stopped to do his business.

"Fine."

"How's..." Sam paused, glanced at her mother, then said, "Joe?"

Did they know? Had Mrs. Morris called Suzanne after all to tell her Joe was in the hospital?

Sam watched me expectantly, like she was waiting for an answer, but Suzanne just gazed out over the moving water. Maybe Sam was just making polite conversation. As in *how are you and how is your family?*

"He's...fine," I said carefully. "I think Sherlock is done now. If you want to leave."

We headed back to the car. Along the way, Sam's phone rang again. "Hello?" she said. She talked to this person in one-syllable words, too. "Yeah...No...No...Maybe." She glanced at me when she said that. *Was she talking about me?* "I don't know. I'll see...Yeah...Yeah! Okay, bye."

By this time we were back at their car. Sam opened the back door and wow, I don't think I've ever seen such a clean car before. There wasn't a speck of dirt anywhere. Not even on the carpet. Sam motioned for me to get in, so I did. I slid all the way across the seat to make room for Sam, then pulled Sherlock onto my lap.

Suzanne put her key in the ignition and we were off. But we didn't even get out of town before Sam's phone rang *again*.

"Wow, you must have a lot of friends," I said.

"Samantha," Suzanne said sharply. "Tell your friends to stop calling and then turn off that phone!"

Whoa. I didn't mean she shouldn't talk to her friends; I just meant that if I had a cell phone, it wouldn't ring nearly as often as hers did. But whatever. I patted my dog's back and turned to look out the window.

"I can't talk right now," Sam said in a low voice. "Yes...Yes...Okay, bye." She clapped the phone closed and I heard the chime sound as it shut off.

Now no one was saying anything. Which was worse than when Sam's cell phone kept ringing. At least then it wasn't so obvious that the three of us were total strangers who didn't know what to say to each other.

Sherlock crawled out of my lap and inched his way over to Sam's side of the car. She eyed him warily.

"He won't hurt you," I said. "He's just checking you out."
Sam smiled weakly.

"Are you hungry, T.J.?" Suzanne asked a little too cheerfully. She glanced at me through the rearview mirror. I couldn't tell for sure, but I got the impression she didn't like seeing Sherlock up on the seat, so I pulled him back onto my lap.

"I don't know. Maybe a little." I should have been hungry. I hadn't eaten since the bus stopped for a break in Mason City. But my stomach was turning somersaults.

"I had thought we'd stop at a restaurant here in Cedar Rapids before heading back," Suzanne said. "But maybe we'd better go all the way to Clearwater first, so we can drop your dog off."

"Aw," Sam groaned. "We don't have a Red Lobster in Clearwater."

"No, but we have other restaurants," Suzanne said. "What do you like, T.J.?"

"Anything," I said. "I'm not picky. Except for eggs. I don't like eggs." Hopefully Suzanne wouldn't make me a nice big scrambled egg breakfast tomorrow.

"Do you like crab legs?" Sam asked.

"I don't know. I don't think I've ever had them."

"You've never had crab legs?" Sam shrieked.

"Well, maybe once. A long time ago. I don't remember." I was virtually positive I'd never had crab legs.

"Crab legs are my favorite," Sam said. "What's your favorite food?"

"Chili cheese burritos," I said. When Sam looked at me blankly, I added, "From Taco Bell."

"Oh," Sam said. "We don't go to Taco Bell very much."

Well, I didn't go to Red Lobster very much. In fact, I wasn't sure I'd ever been to a Red Lobster.

Sam and I kept sort of glancing at each other out the corners of our eyes, but we were both trying not to be obvious about it. I wondered if she was thinking the same thing I was: *This girl is my sister?* It was pretty obvious we weren't anything alike. For one thing, she was a girly girl; I wasn't. We hadn't been on the road ten minutes before she whipped out a comb and small mirror from her purse. I don't even own a mirror or a purse.

"My hair is such a mess!" she whined.

"Looks fine to me," I said. I saw Suzanne smile a little in the rearview mirror.

Sam spent the next fifteen minutes fussing with her hair, and even then she still wasn't happy. "You're so lucky you have short hair," she said to me. She examined herself in her tiny mirror, moving it up and down to get a look at herself from all angles. "Maybe I should cut my hair like yours?"

She had to be kidding. There'd be no telling us apart if she did that. "I'm actually thinking of growing mine out," I said.

"Really?" Sam squealed.

"Yeah," I said, though I had absolutely no intention of growing my hair out. I use Joe's clippers and shave it down every few weeks. It's easy to deal with, and well…Joe and I don't have money for regular haircuts.

"I think you'd look nice with longer hair, T.J.," Suzanne put in. "Of course you wouldn't have to wear it as long as

Sam's, just long enough to frame your face a little. Give you more of a feminine look."

"I'll think about it," I said. I was tired of talking about hair.

But none of us could come up with anything else to talk about, so we rode in awkward silence for the next few miles. I wondered how much longer it would be until we got to Clearwater. I felt like the weird new relative that nobody knew how to deal with. Of course, I *was* the weird new relative nobody knew how to deal with.

Sam reached over and patted the top of my dog's head. "Your dog's name is Sherlock, right?" she asked. "Just like my cat."

"Yeah," I said.

"That's so bizarre that we both named our pets Sherlock." Sam smiled as my dog licked her hand.

"Coincidence," I said.

"You think it's a *coincidence* we both named our pets Sherlock?"

"What else could it be?"

"Well," she smiled. "We're twins, aren't we? Twins usually have a kind of psychic connection between them."

Sure. Whatever.

More awkward silence. But I was starting to see signs for motels, fast food restaurants, and gas stations in Clearwater now. Twelve miles ahead. Then seven miles. Then two miles.

"Here we are," Suzanne announced as we passed the city limits sign.

Population 8,245. I'd never lived in a town that small.

Not that I remembered, anyway. I had, of course, lived the first three years of my life right here. But nothing looked or felt at all familiar to me. I stared out the window as we passed a car dealership...a Hardee's and a Pizza Hut...a bank...a school.

"Is that where you go to school?" I asked Sam. Was that where *I* would've gone to school if—

"No. That's the Catholic school," Sam said.

We turned into a residential neighborhood. The houses were newer than the houses in Gram's neighborhood. Suzanne made two more turns, then pulled up in front of a small two-story blue house with a **FOR SALE** sign in the middle of the yard.

"This is where we live," Sam said.

"For another four days anyway," Suzanne said, turning off the ignition.

We all got out of the car, but I just stood there with Sherlock and all my stuff and stared at the house. It was bigger than Gram's house. Cheerier, too. But that was only because there were flowers out front.

"This is where—" The words caught in my throat.

"Where you used to live?" Suzanne finished for me. "Yes."

I had no memory of that. None whatsoever.

Chapter Eight

It may have been a mistake to let Sherlock off his leash when we got inside the house. The biggest cat I'd ever seen in my life popped out from behind the couch and started prowling around him.

I am not a cat person, but Sherlock walked right over to that cat and tried to make friends with it. The cat arched his back and hissed.

"Sherlock!" Sam and I both screamed at the exact same time. I looked at her and she looked at me. *That was weird.*

My dog dropped to the floor and lowered his head in shame, but no one was mad at him. It was that stupid cat. Sam tried to grab her cat, but he slipped out of her grasp and scurried away.

"It may take a while for the two of them to get used to each other," Suzanne said. "Our Sherlock isn't used to dogs."

"And my Sherlock isn't used to cats," I said, trying to comfort my dog.

"They'll be fine once they get to know each other," Sam said. "So does this house seem more familiar now that you're inside? I mean, do you kind of remember living here?"

"Not really," I said. I glanced around the small living room, taking in the piles of moving boxes, the brown couch, the end tables. Their furniture looked a lot nicer than our furniture. I paused when noticed the wooden rocking chair.

Did Suzanne rock me in that rocking chair when I was a baby? Did Joe?

"We'll show you around real quick and then you can put your things in the den," Suzanne said. "That's where you'll be sleeping. Would you like to change before we go out to eat?"

I looked down at my white shirt and cut-offs. They were old, but they were clean. "Do you want me to change?" I asked.

"It's up to you," Suzanne said. "I think we'll probably just go grab a pizza."

Well, if it was up to me, I wasn't changing. "I'm fine," I said.

"Maybe once you've seen the rest of the house, it'll start to feel more like home," Sam said.

Home? Not likely, I thought as I picked up my duffel bag.

Sam and Suzanne gave me a quick tour of the first floor. Beyond the living room was your basic kitchen, bathroom, and family room. Every room except the bathroom was piled with boxes.

They led me up the stairs to a hallway piled with even more boxes. Jeez! How much stuff did these people have? When Joe and I moved in with Gram, everything we owned fit in the camper on the back of our truck.

The upstairs walls were bare, but I could tell by the holes in the walls that there used to be pictures hanging on both sides of the hallway. Lots of pictures.

Suzanne stopped abruptly in front of a closet. "I want to show you something, T.J.," she said.

"Oh! Good idea, Mom," Sam said as Suzanne slowly opened the door to the linen closet. They both stood back to watch my reaction.

I didn't get it. The closet was empty.

"Look," Sam gestured toward the inside of the door. "Proof that you lived here."

I stepped closer and peered at the door. There were pencil marks on it. Two columns of them. The marks in the outside column started at about my thigh level and went three quarters of the way up the door. They were labeled "Sam: 9 months," "Sam: 15 months," "Sam: 18 months," etc., all the way up to 13 years. Which reminded me, *I was thirteen, too. Not twelve.*

There were fewer pencil marks in the other column. They started at about the same place as the first marks, but they stopped below the doorknob. They were labeled like the other one—"Sarah: 9 months," "Sarah: 15 months," "Sarah: 18 months," "Sarah: 2 years," "Sarah: 2 $^1/_2$ years," and "Sarah: 3 years."

I bent down to take a closer look and my duffel bag fell off my shoulder. I touched the tip of my finger to the

"Sarah: 3 years" mark. Was this *me?* Was this was how tall I was when Joe took me away?

"You used to love to get measured," Suzanne said. "You had a toy tape measure and you'd bring it to me and say, 'Mommy measure.'"

Joe and I never lived anywhere long enough to mark how tall I was on the inside of a door. I had no idea how tall I was when I was six or seven or ten years old.

Does it really matter? I asked myself. Suzanne and Sam were moving out of this house in four days. They weren't going to take the door with them, so after this week, no one would ever remember how tall Sam was when she was six or seven, either.

I stood up and grabbed my duffel bag. "Well, where did you want me to put this?" I asked.

"That's the den right behind you," Suzanne said.

"My room's right next door," Sam said. "Mom's room is over there." She pointed across the hall. "And the bathroom is across from my room."

"Can I use the bathroom?" I asked.

"Of course," Suzanne said. "You don't have to ask."

I left my duffel outside the den, then went into the bathroom. *It was pink.* Pink walls, pink carpet, pink toilet. Just like the bathroom I saw in my head when Sam showed up at my house. There was a white dish by the sink that had little pink soap pieces that were shaped like shells, and a pink basket with tubes and ointments next to the soap. No ballerina picture on the wall, though. There wasn't anything on any of the walls except a mirror above the sink and two towel racks across from the toilet. *Did I really remember this bathroom?*

No way. I was three years old when I lived here. I couldn't possibly remember anything from that long ago.

When I came out of the bathroom I had a perfect view right into Sam's room. She wasn't in there, but man, she was a slob. Like Joe. She had clothes, books, papers, and shoes strewn all over her unmade bed, a pile of boxes, and the floor. A fancy blue dress hung from the top of her closet door. Whoa. My black dress pants weren't going to look very dressy next to that. But that was okay. At least they'd be comfortable.

Suzanne came up behind me. "Would you like to call your dad before we go to dinner?" she asked. "To let him know you got here okay?"

I did want to call him, more than anything. But not in front of Suzanne. "Can I call him when we get back?" I asked.

"Of course," Suzanne said. She actually looked a little relieved. "I think we're all pretty hungry."

I followed her down the stairs and found Sam sitting on the floor petting her cat with one hand and my dog with the other. My Sherlock didn't normally like strangers, but he sure seemed to like Sam. He was licking her hand and everything.

"Are we going now?" Sam asked, pulling herself to her feet. Sherlock sniffed her ankles and sort of danced around her, wagging his tail like he wanted to know where we were all going.

"Yes," Suzanne said. She grabbed her keys from her purse. "Where do you want to go, Sam?"

"I thought we were going for pizza," Sam said. "That's what you said before."

Suzanne looked at me. "Is that okay with you, T.J.?"

"Fine." I shrugged. I didn't really care. I gave Sherlock a good-bye hug and kiss, then followed Suzanne and Sam back out to their car.

The pizza place was decorated in a medieval theme. There were pictures of knights and coats of armor on the wall, and the pizzas had names like the Excalibur and Guinevere's Garden Special. Joe would've loved it. I felt an ache in my chest.

"What's your favorite kind of pizza, T.J.?" Suzanne asked once we all had paper menus.

"I don't really have a favorite," I said. I seriously doubted they'd want to order bacon and pineapple. Most people thought that was weird.

"Can we get bacon and pineapple?" Sam asked. "That's my favorite," she told me.

No way.

"T.J. may not like bacon and pineapple, Sam," Suzanne said.

"No, bacon and pineapple is fine," I said, staring at my menu.

When the waitress came back, we ordered a large bacon and pineapple. Then we were out of things to talk about again. Was it going to be like this the whole week? Nobody knowing what to say?

"So," I said, patting my hands against the table. "What

all is going to happen while I'm here? I know you're getting married on Saturday and I know you're moving on Sunday. Is there anything else I need to know?"

Suzanne and Sam looked at each other. "Well, my folks are coming tomorrow," Suzanne told me. "They live in Florida, so we'll have to go back to Cedar Rapids and pick them up at the airport. Do you remember your Grandma and Grandpa Sperling?"

I had a Grandma and Grandpa Sperling? "No," I said, slurping my pop. But as soon as I said it, I flashed on this huge, burly guy with whiskers who used to let me stand on his feet and we'd walk around the room like that. Was that Grandpa Sperling? Or was that Grandpa Wright, Gram's husband? Grandpa Wright died when I was little, so it could have been either one.

"Well, you'll meet them tomorrow," Suzanne said. Her smile seemed a little strained. "They'll be staying at the house with us, so they'll be there with you and Sam Saturday night when Bob and I are at the hotel."

If I remembered right, Bob was The Fiancé.

"And lucky you," Sam said, patting my arm. "You'll get to meet all of Bob's relatives tomorrow, too."

"Oh, that's right," Suzanne said. "Mom's having everyone over for a barbecue tomorrow night."

"At your house?" I said, wondering just how many people *everyone* was. I also wondered whether Grandma Sperling knew about all the boxes that were piled all over Suzanne's house. Where were they going to put everyone for this barbecue?

"She calls Bob's mother 'Mom,'" Sam explained. "Bob's

mother is the one having everyone over tomorrow. Not Grandma Sperling."

Oh.

"I know, it's weird," Sam said, rolling her eyes.

Suzanne frowned at Sam. "It shows I think of her as family," she said tightly. "I wish you thought of her that way, too."

Sam slumped back against her chair. "Do we have to go through this again? I keep telling you, it's not like I have anything against her. Or any of them. Why do you have to take it as a personal insult if I don't want to call Bob's mother 'Grandma'? It doesn't mean I don't like her or that I don't want you to marry Bob. It just means she's not my grandma."

I was with Sam. Family wasn't something you could simply turn on when someone else wanted you to. It was something you had to feel.

"Okay, okay." Suzanne held up her hands. "Forget I said anything." She turned to me. "How many dresses did you bring, T.J.?"

"Uh…" *Dresses?*

"Did you bring a separate one for the rehearsal dinner, or were you planning on wearing the same one you're wearing to the wedding?"

I had no idea what a rehearsal dinner was. "I…didn't bring any dresses," I said.

"None?" Suzanne looked like she was about to have a heart attack.

"No," I said slowly. "I…don't have any."

"You don't have any dresses?" Sam cried. Man, you'd think I'd said I didn't have any clothes.

"No." Where did I go that I needed to wear a dress? Nowhere.

"Wow," Sam said, reaching for her drink. "Well, I could unpack some of mine and you can borrow whichever ones you want."

She could unpack *some* of hers?

"No, absolutely not." Suzanne shook her head. "If T.J. doesn't have any dresses of her own, she's not going to wear one of yours, Sam."

Whew! *Thank you, Suzanne.*

"We'll just have to take you shopping," Suzanne added. "Tomorrow."

"That's okay," I said quickly. "I brought my black pants and white dress shirt. They're pretty nice." I really didn't want Suzanne spending lots of money on me. Especially on a dress.

But Suzanne just shook her head. "We're taking you shopping, T.J., and that's final."

Great. The only thing I could think of that was worse than shopping was shopping for a *dress*.

* * *

When we got back to their house, we could hear Sherlock barking before we ever went inside.

"What's the matter with your dog?" Sam asked as Suzanne unlocked the door.

"I don't know," I said. It didn't sound like his I'm-so-happy-you're-home bark; it sounded like something was wrong.

Suzanne pushed open the door and we all crowded inside. Suzanne groaned. There were overturned boxes with coats, boots, shoes, gloves, umbrellas, books, and magazines spilled all over the living room. A small lamp on the table next to the couch had been knocked over. Shards of glass littered the table and the carpet below. And Sherlock was up on his hind legs, barking at their cat, who was sprawled out across the top of a pile of boxes, meowing and batting at my dog.

"Stop it!" Suzanne clapped her hands together and both animals looked at her. "Stop it right now!"

"Hey! Don't yell at my dog!" I cried. This couldn't have been all his fault.

"I'm yelling at both of them," Suzanne said. "They're probably both to blame."

Oh. There wasn't much I could say to that, given the mess and all. So I slunk past Suzanne and picked up my Sherlock. The stupid cat glared at me, then leaped to the floor and padded away.

Suzanne just stood there with her hand to her head, staring at the mess. I felt a little bad about the broken lamp, but there wasn't much anyone could do about it.

"I'll go get the garbage can," Sam said as she started for the kitchen.

"I'll help you," I said, scurrying after her. I didn't want to be stuck here alone with Suzanne. But when we got to the kitchen, we found the garbage can knocked over and most of its contents strewn all over the floor, too. Sam didn't say anything; she just started picking it all up. I set my dog down and helped her.

"Hey, what's that phone number on your hand?" Sam asked.

I quickly closed my fingers over the number so she couldn't see it.

"Is that your boyfriend's number?" She grinned.

Boyfriend? "No, it's…" *The best lies always had an element of truth to them.* "It's the number for the hospital. Um, the hospital where I volunteer."

"You volunteer at a hospital?" Sam asked.

"Yeah," I said. Maybe I would see about volunteering there sometime.

"Cool."

Once we got everything back in the garbage can, we went back to the living room. Sam helped her mom pick up the broken lamp pieces. I didn't really know what to do, so I just started putting random things into random boxes. My dog plopped down on the floor, rested his head on his paws, and watched us all.

Again, nobody was saying anything. We were probably all wishing my dog and I had never come.

"Maybe I should take Sherlock for a walk," I said, eager to get out of there for a while.

Sherlock's ears twitched when he heard the word WALK, but he didn't raise his head.

"That's not a bad idea," Suzanne said.

"I'll go with you if you want," Sam offered.

"That's okay," I said. "I can maybe call Joe while I'm

gone. You know, to let him know I got here okay." Hadn't Suzanne suggested I do that? "Can I borrow someone's cell phone?"

"Sure," Sam said. She reached for her purse, pulled out that pink butterfly phone, and handed it to me.

"Thanks," I said, sliding it into my front pocket.

"Don't be gone too long," Suzanne said. "It's starting to get dark."

"Okay," I said, but I wasn't afraid of the dark. I attached Sherlock's leash to his collar and led him out the door. I could feel the tension draining from my shoulders as soon as the door closed behind me. I needed this walk as bad as my dog.

"Where should we go, boy?" I asked as we strolled down the driveway. The porch light clicked on behind me.

I didn't know this town at all, so I had no idea where to go. But it wasn't like we could actually get lost in a town this size. I pointed Sherlock in the direction that seemed to lead toward the main part of town. Once we got about three blocks away from Suzanne and Sam's house, I pulled out Sam's phone and dialed the number I'd written on my hand.

The phone rang five times before anyone picked up. But whoever picked up never said hello.

"Hello?" I said. "Joe?"

"T.J.? Is that you?" He sounded tired. Or drugged up.

"Yeah, it's me," I said, smiling. I was so happy to hear his voice. "How are you?"

"I'm okay." He sounded happy to hear my voice, too. "How are you? Are you in Iowa?"

"Yeah."

"How's it going?"

"Okay. I don't think they like Sherlock very much, though. We went out to eat and when we got back to their house he had knocked over some boxes and a lamp. The lamp got broken."

"You took Sherlock down there with you?"

"Yeah. What else was I supposed to do with him?"

He paused. "I don't know. I guess I didn't think about that." There was another pause. "What do you think of your mom and Sam?" Joe asked.

"I don't know." I didn't want to talk about them. "How are you doing? Really? Are you getting better?"

"I think so. I'm awfully sore, though."

"Will you be out of the hospital when I get back?"

"I hope so."

I hoped so, too. I knew he wouldn't be back to normal in a week, but as long as he was home, that was the important thing. If he was home, no one could take me away from him.

I wasn't ready to go back to Suzanne's house yet when Joe and I hung up, so Sherlock and I just kept walking. We came to a small downtown area. All the stores were lit up, but nothing was open and no one was out and about. We walked past the downtown area and into another residential neighborhood. This neighborhood was more like Gram's neighborhood. The houses were old and small. I glanced to the right as Sherlock and I crossed a street. I could see a park in the next block, so I steered Sherlock down that way.

It was completely dark out now. And much darker on this street than it was downtown. I didn't mind, though. I liked walking around in the dark. Especially in this town. It made me feel invisible. Which was the opposite of how I felt when I was with Sam and Suzanne.

I crossed over to the park and saw a sad-looking swing set with no swings, a crooked merry-go-round, and way at the far edge of the park was a rocket ship slide. None of the parks near us had those. I played on one when I was little, though. I remember climbing all the way to the top and Joe coaxing me down. I never wanted to come down.

Could that have been *this* rocket ship slide?

I couldn't remember. All I remembered was him standing at the bottom saying, "I'll catch you! I'll catch you!"

And he always did.

I picked my dog up and carried him like a football as I climbed one-handed into the ship. I climbed past the second level where the slide was, all the way to the top. Either these things had gotten a lot smaller, or I'd gotten a lot bigger. There was barely room for me to sit in here anymore. But I squeezed in anyway and sat down with Sherlock in my lap.

I leaned my head against the bar and tried to remember whether I'd ever been to this park before. Had I come here with Joe? Had I come here with Joe, Sam, and Suzanne? We'd all been a family once. That's what everyone said.

But if that was true, how come I couldn't remember?

Chapter Nine

Where have you been?" Suzanne asked the minute I walked in. Sam sort of cowered in the doorway and shot me a glad-I'm-not-you look. She had her nightshirt on already. It was navy blue, just like mine, but hers had a teddy bear on it and mine had a number nine on it.

"Uh...walking Sherlock," I said. Which Suzanne knew. It wasn't like I'd snuck out of the house or anything.

Suzanne checked her watch. "It's eleven twenty."

I didn't have a watch, but yeah, it probably was somewhere around eleven twenty. So what?

"You left more than two hours ago!"

"I like to walk," I said as I took Sherlock's leash off and slung it over the doorknob. I noticed that all the mess in the living room had been cleaned up. "I walked all the way from our house to Calhoun Square a couple of weeks ago. It took me two hours, and that was just one way."

"Does your dad let you walk around by yourself this late at night?"

"Uh—" Was that not a good thing?

"Don't you know what can happen to girls who walk around by themselves after dark?"

In this town? Probably not much. But I didn't want to get into it with Suzanne. "I'll come back earlier next time," I said.

"You'll come back earlier, *and* you'll take Sam with you," Suzanne said.

What? Sam was supposed to be my chaperone now? At least she had the decency to look a little uncomfortable about that.

"Whatever," I said. "Can I go to bed now?" Not that I was tired. I hardly ever went to bed before midnight in the summer.

"Yes," Suzanne said, looking away.

Sherlock and I trudged past the boxes up the stairs. I quick went to the bathroom, then headed down to the den. I was pretty sure I'd left my duffel out in the hall, but some-one had picked it up and brought it into the room. They'd set it on the floor next to the fold-out couch that had been neatly made up with pink-and-white flowered sheets and a pink blanket. A fluffy pink towel and matching washcloth lay on top of the pillow.

Joe and I had never had overnight guests before, but if we did we'd probably just hand them a blanket, a pillow, and the least scraggly towel we could find.

I closed the door and started getting undressed. I could hear Suzanne and Sam talking in hushed voices out in the hall, but I couldn't quite make out what they were saying. Whatever it was, I bet it was about me.

Well, so what? What did I care what they thought of me? I was only here because I had to be. And it was only for a week. Six more full days.

I needed to brush my teeth but I didn't want to have to walk past them and risk getting into another conversation with Suzanne on my way to the bathroom. I held my hand in front of my mouth and breathed into it. My breath wasn't too bad. Maybe I'd just skip brushing my teeth tonight.

I would've turned on the TV for a little bit, if there had been one. All they'd left in the room was an empty desk, a couch, and a bunch of boxes.

I didn't know what else to do besides go to bed. The sheets smelled as flowery as they looked. Our sheets at home didn't smell anything like this. I patted the space beside me a couple times and Sherlock jumped up. He plopped down next to me, his body pressed comfortably against mine.

Suzanne and Sam must have finished their conversation. I heard footsteps moving down the hall. Then I heard a door open and close, a toilet flush, water running, another door close. Finally everything got quiet.

Too quiet.

There was no TV on in the next room, no dogs barking in the distance, no people yelling, no freeway noise, nothing. How was I supposed to sleep without any noise at all?

I wondered if Joe was sleeping right now? Was he sleeping or was he lying awake thinking about me?

I rolled onto my stomach and hugged my pillow to my cheek. A few minutes later, I heard a door open somewhere out in the hall. I watched the bottom of my door for the hall light to come on, but it never did. Then I heard my doorknob start to turn. Sherlock's head popped up.

Someone was coming in.

Who was it? Sam? I was trying to be nice to her. Really, I was. But hanging out together in the middle of the night was going a little above and beyond the call of duty. I closed my eyes and tried to breathe slow and deep like I was asleep. I figured she'd get the hint and leave.

I breathed slow and deep for so long that I began to wonder whether she had slipped out when I wasn't paying attention. I cracked one eye open.

Nope. There was a dark figure leaning against the desk across the room. Watching me. But even in the darkness I could tell it wasn't Sam. It was *Suzanne.*

I quick closed that eye and tried to get control of my breathing. But it's hard to breathe slow and deep when your heart is racing.

What was she doing in here in the middle of the night? Why was she just standing there watching me sleep?

All of a sudden I heard sniffling. Was she...*crying?* That was what it sounded like. Why was she crying?

Sherlock jumped down. I could tell he'd gone over to her. Was he nuzzling up to her?

I didn't know what to do. Or what to say. I hoped Suzanne didn't expect me to say or do anything. I hoped she thought I was actually asleep.

Eventually she left and closed the door behind her. But after that, it took me even longer to fall asleep.

* * *

Suzanne pounded on my door at the crack of dawn. "T.J.? Are you up?" she asked. "We're going shopping this morning, remember?"

I groaned. I wasn't thrilled about the shopping or about being woken up so early. Neither was Sherlock.

"T.J.?" The door opened a crack and Sherlock sat up. "Did you hear me?"

"Yeah," I croaked.

"You should get up. We're going to leave in an hour and a half."

An hour and a half? Then why did I have to get up *now?* But I didn't want to be difficult, especially after last night. So I just said, "Okay." Once Suzanne saw me sit up, she smiled and closed the door. No sign of tears this morning.

I grabbed my shampoo, towel, and clothes and staggered to the bathroom. But the door was closed; someone else was already in there. Probably Sam. I left my stuff on the floor outside the door, took Sherlock outside, then came back. She was *still* in there. I sat down on the floor and waited for the door to open. Sherlock curled up beside me and I put my arm around him.

A few minutes later, Suzanne came by. She glanced down at me and Sherlock with surprise, then frowned at the closed door. She rapped her knuckles sharply against it. "Sam, are you still in there?"

"Yes!"

"What are you doing?"

"Getting ready! What do you think?"

"T.J. needs to get ready, too."

The door opened and Sam peered out at me. She had a brush in one hand and a curling iron in the other. "Oh," she said in a much nicer tone of voice than she'd used with her mom. "Sorry." She yanked the curling iron plug from the socket and came out. "You can have the bathroom now."

"Thanks," I said as I stood up. Sherlock followed me into the bathroom and I closed the door behind him.

"Does that dog go everywhere with you?" Sam asked from the other side of the door.

"Pretty much," I said as I set my stuff down on the counter. Sherlock plopped down on the carpet. I gave his ears a scratch, then turned on the shower.

While I waited for the water to heat up, I rummaged through all the little tubes and bottles of stuff in the basket next to the sink. Lightweight moisturizer. Oil control lotion. Extra emollient night cream. Mineral powder foundation. Soothing eye gel. Liquid eyeliner. I didn't even know what half this stuff was. Or what you did with it. But it must've been important since nobody had packed it yet.

There was more stuff in the shower. One bottle was labeled "2-in-1" body wash and shave. Was that just a fancy way of saying soap? And apple ginseng shampoo? I popped the top on that one and took a whiff. Whoa! Weird. Good thing I brought my own soap and shampoo.

When I came out of the bathroom, Sam was *still* messing with her hair in her room across the hall. I could tell by the way she was sighing and banging her curling iron around that whatever she was trying to do wasn't going so well.

"I really am going to cut my hair," she said when she

noticed me standing in her doorway. "I'm going to cut it all off!"

"Okay," I said, because I didn't know what else to say.

She looked at me. "Do you think I should?"

I shrugged. "If you want shorter hair."

"I don't know." She gathered all her hair in one hand and pulled it away from her face. "I've never had short hair." She peered at her reflection.

"I've never had long hair," I said.

"Yes, you have. When you were little. We both had long hair when we were little."

I took two steps into her room. *Was it once my room, too?* I bet it was. But I couldn't remember.

"Do you remember when we were little?" I asked as I stepped over a pile of clothes on the floor.

"Sort of. It's not hard to remember what you looked like, though. There's always been a picture of you hanging in the hallway."

"There has?"

"Yeah. The last one we have of you. You were three. But we took all the pictures down last weekend and packed them up. You know, because we're moving."

"Oh." I tried to hide my disappointment. It was hard to imagine there was a picture of me hanging on a wall in this strange house. A picture I'd never seen.

"I know where your photo album is, though," Sam said.

"*My* photo album?"

"Yeah. You want to see it?"

"Okay."

I watched as Sam slid a pile of clothes off one of the

boxes and onto her bed. She lifted the flaps on the box and pulled out a couple of photo albums. A postcard fell out of one of them and fluttered to the floor.

I bent to pick it up. It had a picture on the front of a monkey from the San Diego Zoo.

"Hey, we used to live in San Diego," I said. "Joe took me to this zoo." I turned the card over and almost had a heart attack. *For my Sammy Bear. With love from the Monkey Man.* It was definitely Joe's handwriting.

I looked up at Sam. "Joe sent this to you?"

She yanked it out of my hand and tossed it back into the box.

"When did he send it?" I asked.

"A long time ago."

Obviously Joe had thought about her once or twice during those ten years. And I never even knew she existed.

"Do you want to see your photo album or not?" Sam asked as she sat down on her bed. A bound photo album with a white cover rested in her lap. "I found it in the basement a few weeks ago. It's all pictures of you."

I sat down beside her. "How do you know they're not pictures of you?" I asked.

"Because I've seen all my pictures. These are different. Plus my mo—I mean, *our* mom, told me this was your album." Sam opened to the first page and I saw four pictures of a really tiny baby. It looked like the pictures were all taken in the hospital. One showed the whole baby; the next zoomed in on the baby's face. It was sleeping with its little fist curled beside its mouth. The baby was awake in the third picture, though, and in the last one it was crying. Was that baby really *me?*

"Mom always wanted us to have separate identities," Sam explained. "You know, because we're twins. So she started two photo albums. One for you and one for me."

A whole album just for me? It was thick, too. Much thicker than the photo album Joe and I had. And it only had pictures from the first three years of my life.

I turned the page and saw pictures of that same baby lying on a blanket, bundled up in a car seat, sitting on a couch with a younger version of Joe, sitting on a couch with a younger version of Suzanne, squeezed between Joe and Suzanne. Together. They looked…happy. All I could do was stare.

"What are you two doing?" Sam and I both jumped when Suzanne appeared in the doorway. "I told you we need to leave in—" She broke off when she saw what we were looking at.

"I-I'm sorry," I said, snapping the album closed. "I just—" I didn't know how to finish that sentence.

"She wanted to see what she looked like," Sam said. "When she was little."

"It's okay," Suzanne said, her voice softening. She came all the way into the room. "Would you like to—"

"No, I think we're done," I said. I didn't want to look at that album with Suzanne. What if she started crying again?

* * *

I really meant to call Joe after I saw that photo album, but I didn't have a chance. As soon as we'd had breakfast, it was time to go shopping. Suzanne put their cat in the basement this time so he and my dog wouldn't get into things while we were gone. Then we headed out.

It shouldn't have taken as long to find a dress as it did. The mall they took me to wasn't very big. But Suzanne and Sam had to look at every single dress in every single store in the whole mall. Well, every single dress in my size, anyway. They had a system. Suzanne started at one end of the size 7s and Sam started at the other, and whenever one of them saw something they liked, they held it in front of me. If they still liked it, they set it aside for me to try on; if they didn't like it, they put it back. I didn't have to do anything except stand there. Until the pile of dresses got too tall. Then I had to go try them all on.

Suzanne and Sam had something to say about every single one.

"That's a nice cut."

"Yes, but I don't like that shade of green with her eyes."

"This one is close, but…too long…too short…what do you think of this bodice…too lacy…not lacy enough…too old…too young…"

"What do you think, T.J.?" they'd ask me now and then.

I hated them all equally.

"How many more stores are there?" I asked. It boggled my mind that some people actually thought this was fun.

"Not many," Suzanne said. Worry lines creased her forehead. "I don't know what we're going to do if we don't find you something. You've got to have a dress, but we haven't seen anything."

"What are you talking about?" I asked. "We've seen all kinds of dresses. Let's just pick one." What was the big deal?

Suzanne stopped. The way she looked at me I figured I'd said something wrong. She took my hand, led me over to a bench, and gestured for me to sit. "Let me ask you something, T.J.," she said as she sat down on one side of me and Sam sat down on the other. "Would you...like to be a bridesmaid in my wedding?"

"What?" Where did that come from?

"Sam's a bridesmaid," Suzanne said. "I know you and I don't know each other very well yet, but you're still my daughter. It just doesn't feel right to leave you sitting in the congregation."

It felt right to me. "I really don't think——" I began, but Suzanne talked right over me.

"I wanted to ask you to be a bridesmaid a couple of weeks ago, but I wasn't sure how you'd feel about it," she said. "And Bob's mother already made all the bridesmaid dresses. It took her weeks. There's no way she'd have time to make another one for you. But who says bridesmaids all have to wear the same dress?"

"Nobody," Sam said, getting into the spirit of things. "I think it's a great idea."

She and Suzanne both looked at me expectantly.

I didn't know what to say. Like Suzanne said, we hardly knew each other. I didn't want to be her bridesmaid. But somehow Suzanne and Sam took my silence to mean *yeah, I'd love to be a bridesmaid.*

"We need to start over and look at more formal dresses," Sam said.

Start over?

"Von Mauer had some nice formal dresses," Suzanne said. "Let's go back there."

"Don't we have to go to the airport?" I asked.

"Yes," Suzanne said. "So we're going to have to do this quick."

We hustled back to Von Mauer and made a beeline for their formal section. This time I just stayed in the dressing room while Sam brought me a new pile of dresses to try on.

"Nope," Sam said after each one.

Nope. Nope. Nope.

I was about to tell her that some people just don't look good in dresses and that we probably were never going to find one, when all of a sudden she squealed, "That's it! That's the dress!"

I looked down at myself. I was wearing this shiny hot pink thing. *Hot Pink.*

"Let me go get my mom," Sam said.

Suzanne had two more dresses draped over her arm when she came back with Sam, but as soon as she saw me she stopped. "Oh, my," she said, her eyes fixed on me. "I think you're right, Sam. We found the dress."

Whatever. At least we were done.

"Hey, Mom?" Sam said in a small voice.

"Hmm?" Suzanne walked slowly around me, checking

out the dress from all angles. I wasn't sure she was even listening to Sam.

"There's another dress just like this one out there," Sam said. "Could we get it for me?"

Was she kidding? She actually *wanted* to wear this dress? Suzanne looked at Sam. "For the wedding?"

"Yes. Then T.J. and I will match."

Oh, boy. We could be...twins!

"I don't know," Suzanne said. "Bob's mother made you that other dress. She worked very hard on it."

"Well, it's not like I'm going to throw it away. I'll wear it some other time. Don't you think it would be nice if T.J. and I wore the same dress?"

Not that I wanted to be Sam's twin, but if I had to be in this wedding, it would be better if I wasn't the only one wearing a dress that was different from everyone else's.

"Bob's mother would understand," Sam insisted.

I looked at Suzanne. I could tell she was thinking about it. "Well, let's see if it fits," she said. "Then we'll decide."

Sam ran over to get the dress and was back in record time. I moved away from the dressing room so she could get changed. About seven seconds later, she slid the curtain open. "It's perfect!" she declared.

"All right," Suzanne said. "We'll get both of them."

Then there was the matter of the shoes. Apparently, when you bought a hot pink dress you needed hot pink shoes to go with it. Who knew stores even sold hot pink shoes? But Von Mauer sold them. And they had two pairs that fit Sam and me.

"See? This was meant to be," Sam said as she paraded in front of the mirror in her new shoes. I'd already taken mine off and put them back in the box.

"Perhaps we should get you a new pair of tennis shoes while we're here, too, T.J.?" Suzanne said as I slipped back in to my old ones.

"Why?" I asked. There was only one little hole in my right shoe. In fact, it was so small it had to be raining really hard before my foot got wet. "I don't need any," I said. I certainly didn't need Suzanne to buy me new shoes.

"Oh, I think you do," she said.

"Totally," Sam agreed, scrunching up her nose.

"What brand do you like, T.J.?" Suzanne peered closer at my feet. "Are those Nikes? That's what Sam gets."

Nikes? Was she kidding? "They're whatever was cheap at Wal-Mart last September," I said.

"Well, why don't you go pick out a pair of Nikes that you like?" Suzanne said.

"I really don't—"

"Please, T.J." Suzanne put up her hand to stop my arguing. "Let me do this for you. Let me buy you some shoes."

She was already buying me shoes. And a dress.

But whatever. If she really wanted to buy me some Nikes, I would let her. That would be twenty bucks Joe wouldn't have to spend on shoes before school started. I went over to the tennis shoe display and picked out the cheapest pair of Nikes I could find. They were still sixty-five bucks. I found my size and brought the box over to Suzanne.

"Don't you want to try them on?" Sam asked.

All of a sudden I remembered another pair of shoes. Pink shoes with little flowers all around the top and a strap with a buckle. And a lady's voice: *I know you want these, Sarah, but we have to try them on first. We have to make sure they fit.*

The Nike box slipped through my fingers and clattered to the floor.

"What's the matter?" Sam asked, looking at me curiously as she picked up the shoes and handed them to me.

"Nothing," I said, feeling a little shaky. Did that really happen? Did I really want a pair of pink shoes with flowers when I was little? Was that Suzanne who told me I had to try them on first?

"You should try them on," Suzanne said, nodding at the shoes in my hand. "Nike's sizes sometimes run a little different than other shoe brands."

Did I ever get the pink shoes with the flowers?

I sat down on the floor and tried on the Nikes. Suzanne was actually right about the sizes. I always wore a size 6 in shoes. But the size 6 Nikes did seem a little tight. The size 7 felt good, though. In fact, they were the most comfortable shoes I'd ever had on my feet. I wasn't sure I'd actually be able to save them until school started next month.

"Thanks for buying me all this stuff," I told Suzanne while she paid.

She smiled at me. "Thank you for letting me buy you all this stuff."

Chapter Ten

I didn't believe Sam when she said the Cedar Rapids airport was in the middle of a cornfield, but that's exactly where it was. Out in the middle of nowhere, south of town, surrounded by cornfields.

We parked and went in through the sliding glass doors, then rode the escalator up to a big lobby. Various ticket counters lined the room. Northwest Airlines, United Airlines, Delta Airlines, Hertz Rent-a-Car. There was even a restaurant and a gift shop that sold Iowa souvenirs.

"We'll have to wait here," Suzanne said. "They won't let us go through security without boarding passes." So we found three chairs in the middle of the lobby. Sam and Suzanne sat down next to each other; I took a chair across from them.

Sam pulled out her comb and started messing with her hair. Suzanne smiled uneasily at me. I watched the clock.

I wouldn't say I felt nervous sitting there. Just out of place. Like I had somehow been planted in the middle of someone else's life. Here I was at a strange airport, sitting with a mother and sister I hardly knew, waiting for grandparents I didn't know at all. How many other strangers would I have to deal with over the next couple of days?

"Do you have any brothers or sisters?" I asked Suzanne.

"No," Suzanne said. "I'm an only child."

Oh. *Like Joe,* I thought.

"You didn't know that?" Sam asked.

How would I know that? "Do you know how many brothers and sisters Joe has?" I shot back.

She turned to her mother.

"He doesn't have any, either," Suzanne told Sam.

"Really?" Sam's eyes widened.

I was also a little surprised that neither Joe nor Suzanne had any brothers or sisters. Even if we had all been one big happy family, Sam and I still would never have had any aunts, uncles, or cousins. How many people in the world have zero aunts, uncles, and cousins?

"Well, he used to have a sister," Suzanne said suddenly.

"What?" I said. *No, he didn't.*

Suzanne looked surprised. "He didn't tell you about Katie?"

Katie? "Oh, sure," I said with a shrug. I didn't want Suzanne to know there was something else Joe had never told me. "I just forgot."

"Wait a minute. Who's Katie?" Sam asked, her eyes darting back and forth between me and Suzanne.

"I just told you." Suzanne shifted in her chair and something changed in her voice. "She was your dad's sister. She died when we were teenagers."

"How?" Sam asked.

I wanted to know that, too.

But before Suzanne could respond, a woman's voice came over the loudspeaker. "Announcing the arrival of Northwest flight 671 from Minneapolis at gate C."

Suzanne rose from her chair. "I'll tell you about it later," she told Sam.

"Why can't you tell me now?" Sam asked as we joined the crowd that was gathering in front of the security area.

"Because now is not the time," Suzanne said tightly. "And whatever you do, don't bring Katie up in front of Grandma and Grandpa Sperling."

"Why not?" Sam asked.

Suzanne looked tired. "Just don't, okay?"

"O-*kay!*" Sam said with a heavy sigh.

My eyes met Sam's for just a second, but then I turned away. Inside, though, I was wondering the same thing she was. What was the big deal? Why couldn't Suzanne just quick tell us how Katie died? And why did she warn Sam not to bring Katie up in front of Grandma and Grandpa Sperling? It wasn't like she was *their* daughter. She would've been Gram's daughter. *And Gram never mentioned her, either.*

People were starting to come down the stairs and the escalator on the other side of the security gate now. I saw Suzanne take a deep breath and paste a fakey-looking smile on her face when this lady in a yellow pantsuit who had hair the color of Suzanne's waved at us from the stairs. She wasn't carrying anything except a purse, but the mostly bald guy behind her had an overnight bag in one hand and a duffel bag slung over his shoulder.

Grandma and Grandpa Sperling?

Apparently.

"Hello, Mom. Dad," Suzanne said stiffly. She and the woman in yellow sort of air hugged.

"How are you, Sam?" The guy with all the luggage held out a hand for her to shake.

"I'm fine, Grandpa. How are you?" Sam asked.

Grandma Sperling sidestepped over to me. She was about half an inch shorter than me and she reeked of hair-spray and perfume. "You must be Sarah," she said as she inspected me from head to toe.

"Actually, I go by T.J. now," I said. She didn't offer her hand to shake, so I didn't offer mine, either.

"Hmph," Grandma Sperling sniffed. "Your name is Sarah. That's what your birth certificate says, so that's what I'm going to call you."

"Mother," Suzanne said sharply.

But I didn't need her fighting my battles. "Lots of peo-ple go by names that aren't on their birth certificates," I pointed out.

"Hmm," Grandma Sperling said. "You're a mouthy one, aren't you?"

Just because I want her to call me what everyone else calls me, I'm "mouthy"?

"Let's go get your bags," Suzanne said, quickly leading us all toward baggage claim.

It took forever to get their bags. They had five of them. Five bags for two people. There wasn't room for that much luggage in Suzanne's trunk. Not with all the stuff we'd bought at the mall, too.

"Maybe we can unclip the garment bag and open it up and lay it across the top," Grandma Sperling suggested as she reached for the clips on the bag that was folded over.

Ah. So that *was a garment bag.*

Suzanne laid it across the other big suitcases in the trunk, but the carry-on bags and the packages from the mall had to go in the car with us. Grandma Sperling took one of the bags into the front seat with her; everything else ended up in the backseat with Sam, Grandpa Sperling, and me.

"So, tell us about yourself, Sarah," Grandma Sperling ordered once we were on the way back to Clearwater.

At first I wasn't going to answer any question that was directed at "Sarah." That wasn't my name. But Grandma Sperling actually turned around in her seat and waited for me to answer.

Make them think I raised you right, Joe had told me.

"I don't know what you want to know," I said, looking down at my feet.

"Are you a good student?"

"Yes."

"How good?"

"I get mostly A's."

"Really?" Sam asked.

I shrugged. It wasn't that hard to get A's.

I don't think Grandma Sperling was as impressed as Sam was. She moved on to her next question. "What's your favorite subject?"

"Science."

"Are you in any after-school activities?"

"I'm in band."

"What do you play?"

"The tuba."

That got Grandpa Sperling's attention. "Is that right? I used to play the tuba. Many years ago in high school and college."

"Cool," I said.

"Why in the world would a young girl want to play the tuba?" Grandma Sperling asked.

Because Gram wanted me to play in band and the tuba was the only instrument the school had that they could let me borrow for free. But I wasn't going to tell her that. "I just like it," I said. And I did. Sort of.

"Let's not interrogate T.J., Mother," Suzanne said as she changed lanes. At least *she* called me T.J. "We'll have plenty of time to get to know her over the next few days."

"Well, I don't know about that," Grandma Sperling said, turning back around. "We've got a wedding to get ready for. Is everything in order?" Now all the attention was on Suzanne. Grandma Sperling wanted to know if Suzanne had checked in with the minister. Had she talked to the florist? Was she sure she wanted roses? Roses were so "commonplace." And if she and Suzanne went in tomorrow maybe the florist could still do something different?

"We can't change the order the day before the wedding, Mother," Suzanne said. "Besides, I like roses."

While Grandma Sperling and Suzanne continued to argue about flowers in the front seat, Grandpa Sperling showed Sam and me a bunch of magic tricks. They were pretty lame. Any idiot could see he had a fake deck. And obviously he stuck the little chicken in Sam's purse when she wasn't looking; he didn't just make it appear there out of the blue. But I had no idea how he put the eight torn-up dollar bill pieces that were closed in my fist back together while they were still in my fist. That one was pretty cool.

"I don't suppose you'd show me how you did that?" I said, turning the dollar bill all around.

He smiled. "A magician never reveals his secrets. But since we're related, maybe I'll share just this one with you before I go back home."

"That's okay," I said. "You don't have to tell me."

We were supposed to go over to The Fiancé's mother's house for dinner, but Grandma Sperling wanted to stop back at Suzanne's first to freshen up and drop off their things. Fine with me. That way I could let Sherlock outside before we left.

Suzanne parked in the driveway and popped the trunk.

I grabbed my dress and my new shoes and headed for the front door while everyone else helped with Grandma and Grandpa Sperling's bags. Suzanne unlocked the door and Sherlock stood there barking and wagging his tail in greeting.

"Good heavens!" Grandma Sperling stopped short in the doorway. "When did you get a dog?" She held her bag like a shield between her and Sherlock.

"He's not ours," Suzanne said as she moved to the middle of the living room. "He's T.J.'s."

I dropped my bag of shoes on the floor, laid my dress

over the back of the couch, and went to pick up my dog.

"You brought your dog?" Grandma Sperling wrinkled her nose when Sherlock licked my face.

I ignored the wrinkly nose. "Yes."

"Why?"

I shrugged. "I felt like it."

"It's fine, Mother," Suzanne said as she adjusted her grip on one of Grandma Sperling's suitcases. "We don't mind."

Grandpa Sperling set one suitcase down, then slowly bent to scratch Sherlock's back. "He looks like a nice little dog."

Grandma Sperling pressed her lips together. "Do you always do whatever you feel like doing, *Sarah?*" she asked me.

"T.J.," I corrected her again. "And yeah, pretty much." Man. What was her problem?

"Guess what her dog's name is," Sam said, worming her way in next to her grandma.

Grandma Sperling didn't even try to guess.

"It's Sherlock," Sam said cheerfully. "Just like our cat. Isn't that cool?"

"I suppose," Grandma Sperling agreed.

"It's because T.J. and I are twins. We have a psychic connection," Sam said.

Again with the psychic stuff? I hardly knew the girl.

"Come on, Mother," Suzanne said, heading through the kitchen. "I know you hate climbing stairs so I set up the air mattress for you and Dad in the family room."

"Oh, I don't know if I can sleep on an air mattress," Grandma Sperling muttered as she and Grandpa Sperling followed Suzanne.

"I need to get something upstairs before we go," Sam told me. She raced up the stairs two at a time.

That left me and my dog alone.

I couldn't help but notice that with the cat locked up, there were no broken lamps or overturned garbage cans in the house this time.

"Come on, boy," I said, setting Sherlock down. "Let's go outside."

He scampered through the kitchen and waited for me at the back door. As I walked past the phone, I wondered if I dared grab it and try to make a quick call before we left for the picnic? I wanted to call Joe and see how he was doing, but even more I wanted to ask him about the sister he'd never told me about. Which meant this wasn't likely to be a quick call. It would be better to call later, when I had more time.

I went out into the backyard with Sherlock and watched as he ran around the yard, sniffing for the perfect spot to go. A slight breeze rippled through the trees. As I strolled past the open family room window, I heard Grandma Sperling's voice. "—not quite what we expected, is she?"

Excuse me? I moved closer to the window so I could hear better.

"I didn't have any expectations," Suzanne replied.

"Well, considering where she's been the last ten years, it was probably wise not to expect much."

"I didn't say—"

"She has no manners, no sense of style, and that hair! She looks like a boy."

The screen door slammed behind me and I turned. "Hey," Sam said as she stepped out into the yard.

"Hey," I said, walking quickly toward her. I didn't want her to hear her grandma bad-mouthing me.

"In case you hadn't noticed, Grandma Sperling is a little uptight," Sam said.

"Oh, I noticed," I said.

"And Mom gets a little uptight whenever she's around."

"Noticed that, too," I said, and we both smiled.

"So," Sam said as we followed Sherlock around the yard. "What can you tell me about Katie?"

I groaned to myself. *I should have known Sam would ask me that.* "Not much."

The back door opened then and Suzanne poked her head out. "Time to go, girls."

Whew. Saved by Suzanne. I shrugged helplessly at Sam.

"Tell me later," she said. "After the barbecue."

"Sure," I said.

Maybe in the next couple of hours I'd suddenly remember Joe mentioning something—anything—about a person named Katie.

Chapter Eleven

I knew The Fiancé had a pretty big family, but I had no idea it was this big. I shook hands with Bob's brother Dan, Dan's wife Becky, and their kids Brenna (age 5) and Austin (age 7). Bob's sister Caryn introduced herself, her husband Josh, and their son, Cody (age 6). Bob's brother Rick, who wasn't married, had a 6-year-old son named David...not to be confused with Bob's *brother* David, who was next in line. Then there was David's wife Jenna and their three kids—Katherine (age 7), Karsten (age 5), and Caleb (age 1). And after them Bob's sister Lynne, her husband Tim, and their kids Connor (age 8), Elizabeth (age 6), and Max (age 3). I was never going to remember all of these people.

I wasn't likely to forget Bob's mother, though. She was the last person I met, and she didn't shake my hand. She grabbed me and hugged me. For some reason I didn't mind her hug as much as I minded Suzanne's.

"I'm so glad to meet you, T.J.," she said, holding onto my hands.

She was? I wondered what she'd been told about me.

"Now, you can call me Pauline or you can call me Mrs. Hager or you can call me Grandma or Nana. Whatever you want is fine." She leaned closer to me and whispered just loud enough for me and Sam to hear her: "You can even call me 'Bob's mother' if you want. That's what Sam calls me."

Sam's face turned bright red.

I grinned. "Okay," I said. I liked the idea of calling her "Bob's mother."

Sam and I inched over toward the couch so Suzanne could introduce Grandma and Grandpa Sperling to Bob's mother. I noticed Sam looked kind of stiff and uncomfortable around these people, which surprised me. She wasn't meeting them for the first time today like I was. And they seemed all right to me. At least they weren't all concerned about my hair, my manners, or my "sense of style."

"We've got hamburgers and hot dogs in the kitchen," Bob's mother announced, clasping her hands together. "T.J.? Sam? Are you hungry? Please, go get something to eat."

I didn't need to be told twice; I headed for the kitchen. Sam followed me.

Whoa. Plates of hamburgers, hot dogs, bratwurst, and chicken covered one counter, along with buns, ketchup, mustard, mayo, and a whole bunch of other sauces. Bowl after bowl of pasta and other salads lined the opposite counter. There was even a watermelon that was cut open all fancy and filled with balls of fruit. And the kitchen table was crowded with desserts. I'd never seen so much food in one place before. I grabbed a paper plate and started to help myself to a little bit of everything.

Sam snorted behind me. "You can come back for seconds, you know," she said.

"I might have to," I said, dumping a scoop of pasta and pepperoni on my plate. I was running out of room on my plate already.

Sam shrugged. "Whatever. One thing I can say for these people, they do know how to cook."

Yeah. I sort of got that.

We grabbed napkins, plastic forks, and bottles of pop, then we took all our stuff out through the sliding glass door. There was a big picnic table in the middle of the deck, but Sam and I headed for a couple of chairs at the far end.

"Can you believe all these people?" I asked as I stuck my wad of chewed gum on the edge of my plate. I'd only seen family gatherings like this one on TV. "I wonder what it's like around here at Christmastime."

"Loud," Sam replied.

"You've been here for Christmas?"

"Unfortunately, yes. It's pretty crazy. Everyone opens all their presents at once, so in a matter of seconds the whole living room is covered with wrapping paper and empty boxes. Then, while the parents are cooking dinner, all the kids fight over their new toys and everyone starts crying."

It actually sounded kind of nice to me. Except for the everyone-starts-crying part. My Christmases with Joe were always pretty quiet. There were never enough presents to cover a living room chair, much less a floor. And before we moved in with Gram, we never cooked Christmas dinner.

We always found a church that had free food and we ate there. It was never very good, though. The turkey was always dry, the potatoes runny, and the green beans mushy. I bet they never had dry turkey around here.

"They seem like a really close family," I said. I watched through the glass door as moms and dads dished up food for all those little kids.

"Yeah, I guess," Sam said, stirring the pasta around on her plate.

"What?" I asked. "Do you feel weird around them because you're kind of the outsider?"

"No. That's not it."

A bunch of dads and kids came outside with plates of food. They all spread out in small groups around the picnic table, on the deck stairs, and under trees out in the yard.

Since we weren't alone anymore, Sam leaned over and whispered, "It's like I said at the pizza place yesterday. Mom just keeps pushing all these people on me. She thinks it's so great that we're getting this whole extended family, and now she wants to do *everything* with them. That's fine for her, but I hardly know these people. I just don't feel what she feels."

"I...can understand that," I said. I wondered if it ever occurred to Sam that that might be exactly how I felt about her and her mom?

"So, how did they meet, anyway?" I asked as I popped the last bite of my hamburger into my mouth.

Sam's eyebrows shot up. "My mom and Bob? You don't know?"

Why did she think I knew all this stuff about her family?

She leaned toward me again. "They met when you...disappeared. Bob was the cop who came to our house and told us you'd...fallen into the quarry."

I stopped chewing. They met because of me?

"They didn't start going out right away," she went on. "I don't remember when they started dating. But that's how they met."

"Hey!" one of the dads shouted at us from the middle of the yard. Dan, I think his name was. "You two want to play ball?" He held up a fat, red plastic bat. All the dads and kids watched us expectantly.

"No thanks," Sam said right away.

"Oh, come on," one of the other dads said. "We're out-numbered out here. We could use a couple more players on our team."

"No way!" The tallest of the kids spoke up. He held a white plastic ball in his hand. "It's kids against the grown-ups. They're kids, so they're on our team."

"Yeah! They're on our team." A girl with a long blond ponytail stomped her foot.

"I don't know," one of the dads said. "I think they should be on our team. If they play."

"Let's play," I said to Sam.

She looked at me like I was crazy. "Why?"

I shrugged. "Why not?" We were basically done eating. What else was there to do?

"We're like twice as old as all those other kids," Sam whispered.

"So?" I set my napkin and empty Coke bottle on my plate. "You don't have to play if you don't want to, but I'm going to." I clomped down the deck stairs.

"Yay!" the kids cheered. "She's playing!"

A second and a half later Sam followed me, and the kids cheered even louder.

"Will you be on our team?" A little girl in a yellow dress looked up at me with big brown eyes. "I think you should because you're not all growed up yet."

"Yeah," I said, resisting the urge to ruffle her hair. "We'll be on your team." I thought Dan and the other dads needed some competition.

Sam and I went to join the kids behind home plate. Apparently kids bat first around here. "The deck stairs are first base," Dan told everyone. "The maple tree is second. The post with the two bird feeders is third base. And home is right over there." He pointed to a Frisbee someone had placed on the lawn. "Got it?"

"Sure," I said. I hoped third base didn't get knocked over.

The game started and I quickly found out this wasn't the cutthroat kids-against-parents thing that I expected. Those dads weren't even trying! They sort of baby-stepped along behind their giggly kids when the kids were running bases. They missed throws on purpose. Even when Sam and I were up to bat, none of them made any real effort to get the ball. It was insulting.

Bob's brother Rick was the worst. The ball I hit went right to him. He held out his hands to catch it…and the ball dropped right between his open hands and rolled a few feet behind him. "Oops," he said, looking around and pretending he didn't know where the ball was.

"Oh, come on," I said as I stood there at home plate. "Why are you letting us win?" Joe never let me win just because I was a kid. I remember when I was little and Joe always beat me whenever we played Horse. If I got upset, he'd ask, *Do you really want me to let you win, T. J.?* I'd say *yes,* but it didn't matter. He never slacked off just so I could win.

All of a sudden Rick picked up that ball and slammed it over to Bob's brother Tim, who was on first base.

"Looks like you're out, T.J.," Tim said with a grin.

"See? We're not letting you win," Rick put in.

Oh, what? *Now* they were playing for real? But we should've had about twenty-three outs by then, so it was hard to get too mad.

After that they were a little tougher on Sam and me, but they let their kids get away with murder! It was still sort of fun, though. How cool to be in a family where there were actually enough people for a baseball game.

They could be your family, too, a small voice in my head said. But no, they couldn't. My family consisted of me, Joe, and Gram. That was it.

* * *

We got back to Suzanne's house at around nine o'clock. Grandma and Grandpa Sperling went to get ready for bed. I grabbed Sherlock's leash and called, "Here, boy! Want to go for a walk?"

Sherlock bounded down the stairs. He definitely wanted to go for a walk.

"Take Sam with you," Suzanne called.

Was she serious? "How about if I just take Sam's cell phone instead?" I suggested. "That way I can call you if something happens." I'd been hoping to call Joe while I was out walking. I hadn't had a chance to talk to him all day.

"You know the rules, T.J.," Suzanne said.

I sighed. Why was it such a big freaking deal to go off by yourself around here?

"I don't mind going with you," Sam said as I snapped Sherlock's leash to his collar.

No, but maybe *I* minded. Fine. Whatever. "Let's go," I said, heading out the door before Suzanne could tell us how far we could go or how long we could be gone, too.

"Your mom sure has a lot of rules," I told Sam as we started down the street. Sherlock sniffed every yard we passed.

"I don't know," she said. "I don't think she has any more rules than anyone else's mom. Doesn't your dad have rules?"

"Not really," I said as we crossed the street. "Joe trusts me."

We stopped to let Sherlock do his business. Crickets chirped all around us.

"So what's it like living with Joe?" Sam asked. "What's *he* like?"

"He's...great," I said. We started walking again

"You're pretty close?" Sam said.

119

"Oh, yeah," I said. But inside I wondered, *were* Joe and I close? How could you be close to someone who lied to you and kept secrets from you? "What about you and Suzanne? Are you guys close?"

Sam shrugged. "I don't know. There's a lot she won't talk to me about. She's always been that way. Like she would never tell me anything about Joe. She wouldn't tell me what he was like, what he did for a living, nothing. She wouldn't talk about you, either. It was like the two of you never existed. Of course, I know the reason she never talked about you. It made her feel too sad."

I felt like the ground had just dropped out from under me. Talking about me made Suzanne sad? Was that why Gram and Joe had never mentioned Katie? Did it make them too sad to think about her?

"And you saw Mom at the airport," Sam went on. "She was the one who brought up the fact that Joe used to have a sister, but then, *bam!* she didn't want to talk about it anymore."

"Well, that's because your grandma and grandpa's plane got in."

"No." Sam shook her head. "I know my mom. It was more than that. She just didn't want to talk about Joe's sister. And I kind of got the impression you didn't want to talk about her, either. So, what's the big deal? Why doesn't anyone want to talk about this Katie person?"

"I don't know," I said.

"What do you mean you don't know?" she asked. "You know more than I do. I'd never even heard of her before today."

I sighed. "Neither had I," I admitted.

Sam stopped walking. "What?"

"I'd never heard of Katie before today, either."

She just looked at me.

"What? Why are you so surprised? I didn't even know you or your mom existed until three weeks ago. I didn't know Grandma and Grandpa Sperling existed. Why are you surprised I never knew Joe used to have a sister?"

"I'm not," she said quietly. "I'm surprised that you lied to me."

"I didn't lie to you." I threw my hands up in the air, which jerked Sherlock's collar and made him yelp. "I never actually said I knew anything about Joe's sister. I just said I couldn't tell you much about her. And the reason was because I don't know anything. No lie there."

Sam's eyes narrowed. "No, you said you knew about Katie, you just 'forgot' about her."

Was that what I'd said? "I think you're remembering wrong."

"That's what you said," Sam insisted. Her eyes softened. "But I think I know why you said it."

"You do?"

"I think you didn't want Mom or me to know that there's more Joe hasn't told you."

Wait a minute. *Did* we have some sort of bizarre psychic connection?

"Look. You're not the only one who's been lied to, you know," Sam said. "I may have been the one who found you, but I didn't know you really existed until the second I saw you."

Was I supposed to be grateful to her for finding me? As far as I was concerned, I was never lost.

I started walking again, faster this time. But not fast enough to lose Sam. "Wait, T.J.," she called, hurrying after me. "Don't you understand? You're not alone. You and me, we're in this together."

I whirled around. "In what together?" As far as I could tell, she didn't have to worry about Social Services or her dad's broken back or her grandma in a nursing home.

Sam didn't answer at first. "In this…search for the truth," she said finally. "Don't you think it's strange no one ever told either of us about Katie? She would've been our aunt, T.J. The only aunt we ever had. Don't you want to know who she was? Don't you want to know why she died so young? Don't you want to know why no one ever told us about her?"

"Sort of," I admitted.

"Good," Sam said. A slow smile spread across her face. "Because I think I know how we can find answers to all those questions."

"How?"

"How does any other child of divorce get what they want when one parent says no?" she asked.

I had no idea. I'd never really thought of myself as "a child of divorce" before.

"They go to the other parent," Sam said. She reached into her purse, pulled out her cell phone, and handed it to me. "Call Joe, T.J."

I wanted to call Joe. But not in front of Sam.

"You just said you wanted answers, too," she pointed out.

I took the phone, but instead of punching in the hospital number, I punched in our home number. I waited until the answering machine kicked on, then held out the phone so she could hear it, too. "He's not home," I said.

I tried to give her back her phone, but Sam wouldn't take it. "Hang onto it," she said. "You can keep trying."

She didn't need to offer twice. I was happy to hold on to her phone for a while.

Chapter Twelve

Suzanne wanted us to go to bed as soon as we got back to Sam's house. At 10:30. And when Sam tried to protest, Suzanne put her finger to her lips. "Grandma and Grandpa are already asleep."

I looked toward the family room. The lights were out.

"Tomorrow's a big day," Suzanne went on in a low voice as she ushered us up the stairs. "Your grandparents and I have errands to run in the morning—"

"What kind of errands?" Sam stopped on the third step.

"Just a few last-minute wedding details. I want you to finish packing up your room. We've got the rehearsal dinner tomorrow night, the wedding on Saturday, and then the move on Sunday. You've got to get the rest of your things packed, Sam. No more putting it off."

"Can T.J. and I go to the mall while you're running errands?" Sam asked. "Maybe out to lunch, too?"

Suzanne forgot about the low voice. "Did you hear what I just said about packing, Samantha?" she asked, hands on her hips.

"Yes. But it's not going to take all day."

I almost choked. Had Sam seen her room lately?

"T.J. will help." Sam looked at me. "Won't you, T.J.?"

"Uh—"

But Sam didn't wait for my response. "If we get everything in my room boxed up, can we go to the mall?" She was begging now.

I would've rather cleaned the entire house than go back to that mall.

"Only if you get everything packed first," Suzanne said. "And only if you promise you'll be back by three o'clock. They want us at the church by five."

"I know," Sam said. "We'll be back by then. Can we have some money?"

Whoa. I would never ask Joe for money. Not without a reason, anyway.

"All right. Let's see what I've got in my purse," Suzanne said.

Sam grinned at me, then scrambled the rest of the way up the stairs after her mom. I followed a few paces behind them. When we got upstairs, I saw Suzanne's wedding dress hanging from the top of the door. I'd never seen a real wedding dress before. This one had a scooped neck with a ring of lace and tiny white balls. Some of the lace went all the way to the floor. If Suzanne could afford a dress like that, a dress that she'd only wear once, I shouldn't have been surprised she had money to give to Sam for no good reason.

"Don't feel like you have to spend it all," Suzanne said as Sam started to walk away with the wad of cash.

I turned to leave, too, but Suzanne called me back. "Here's a little something for you, too, T.J.," she said, holding out her hand.

I wasn't actually planning to take her money, but I was curious just how much she was offering. Holy cow! "Fifty bucks!" I blurted out. No one had ever given me fifty bucks for no reason before.

Suzanne smiled. "In case you see a blouse or something you want."

Right. Like I would blow fifty bucks on clothes. I should have said no to Suzanne's money. I *wanted* to say no. But if I added it to the money I had left from my one-way bus ticket, I would have enough to buy another one-way ticket home. So I took it.

"Thanks," I said. I felt a little bit guilty.

When I went back to my room, Sherlock was already curled up on my blanket. I got undressed and put on my nightshirt, but I didn't go right to bed. First I pulled out Sam's cell phone and dialed the hospital. It was a good thing I'd memorized the number; it was starting to fade on my hand already.

I waited while the phone rang and rang.

Nobody picked up. Joe was probably asleep. Darn. I'd have to wait until tomorrow to talk to him.

* * *

The next morning I woke to the sound of muffled voices and people walking around downstairs. It was still pretty dark in my room, but when I checked the clock, I was surprised to discover it was already eight thirty. I peeked under the window shade. A light rain was falling outside.

Sherlock hopped down off the couch and went to the door, his tail wagging. But I didn't make any move to go and open the door.

"We'll go outside when they leave," I told him. He let out a little whine.

"It wouldn't hurt to talk to him," I heard Grandma Sperling say in a low voice. Low for Grandma Sperling was still pretty darn loud. "Find out what your options are."

"I know what my options are," Suzanne said. "And I'm happy with the way things are going."

What were they talking about? I went to the door and pressed my ear against it

"You'll be happy putting her back on a bus in a couple of days? Happy to send her back to *him?*"

"She came here with the understanding it would just be for a week—"

"And you let her go with Joe that day with the understanding it would just be for the afternoon," Grandma Sperling countered. "That man doesn't deserve—"

"This isn't about Joe," Suzanne interrupted. "It's about T.J. and what's best for her."

"And you think sending her back to him is for the best?"

"It's what she wants."

"She's a child! She doesn't get to say what she wants."

Excuse me, *child?* I wanted to go down there and tell Grandma Sperling a thing or two about how it was, but even more I wanted to hear what Suzanne said next.

"It's my decision, Mother. And I'm going to handle it my own way. Now, are we running those errands or not?"

I heard a door open and close. Were they gone? I ran to the window and raised the shade just high enough so I could peek out at the driveway. Suzanne and Grandma and Grandpa Sperling were all getting into Suzanne's car. I waited for them to drive away, then I pulled on a pair of shorts, grabbed Sam's cell phone, and took Sherlock out into the backyard.

My whole body was shaking. It sounded like Suzanne had every intention of letting me go home as planned next week, but what if Grandma Sperling kept working on her? What if Suzanne changed her mind? *Joe, you've got to get better*, I thought. *You've got to be ready to fight for me if it comes to that.*

I opened Sam's phone and punched in the number for Joe's hospital room. The light rain soaked into my night-shirt. Just like last night, the phone rang and rang.

It was quarter to nine. Joe shouldn't still be sleeping now. Not even in a hospital. I tried the number again, but there still wasn't any answer. Had they moved him to another room again? Was the phone simply too far out of his reach? Why hadn't I thought to copy down the hospital's main number, too?

Sherlock was done outside so we went back in the house. I wiped my bare feet on the rug and Sherlock shook himself off.

I tried the hospital again. Still no answer.

Why wasn't Joe answering his phone? He hadn't gotten

worse, had he? Who would tell me if he had? Who else even knew I was here?

Mrs. Morris did. She would call and tell me if something bad had happened, wouldn't she?

Or would she wait until I got home to tell me?

I called Joe's room one more time and finally someone answered. But it wasn't Joe. It was a woman. An older woman, it sounded like. An older woman who probably smoked too many cigarettes when she was young.

"Who is this?" I asked.

"Who are you trying to reach?"

"Joe Wright. He's my dad. Is he there?"

"No, I'm sorry. He's not." She didn't offer any other information.

I sat down on the arm of the couch. "Do you know where he is? Did they move his room again? Who is this?" I asked again.

"I'm your dad's roommate's wife." Her voice got all muffled, like she was covering up the receiver. "Do you know where your roommate is?" I heard a man's voice in the background, then the woman came back on. "My husband says they took him for some tests an hour or so ago."

"What kind of tests?" I asked.

"I don't know. Maybe you should talk to one of the nurses." She gave me the main phone number for the hospital and I repeated it over and over in my head so I wouldn't forget it.

"Ask for the fifth floor nurse's station when you call back," the woman said.

"Thanks," I replied. I hung up and called the other number. I had to go through several other people before I got to talk to one of the nurses on the fifth floor. "Can you tell me where my dad is? His name is Joseph Wright, and the lady in his room said he was taken away for some tests."

"Yes, that's right." The nurse sounded distracted, like she was doing something else while she was talking to me.

"What kind of tests?"

"I'm sorry, I can't tell you that."

"Why not?"

"Privacy rules."

"Well, I'm his daughter," I said. They could tell *me* where they took him, couldn't they?

"Sorry," the woman said. "We're not allowed to release patient information to anyone. Not without the patient's consent."

Wouldn't Joe give them permission to tell me what was going on? "Can you just tell me how he's doing? I mean, did something happen? Is he getting worse? Is that why he's having tests?"

"I'm sorry. I cannot release that information."

I sighed. "Well, what information *can* you release?"

"All I can do is confirm that he is a patient here."

"Gee, thanks," I said. Thanks for nothing.

Now what was I supposed to do? Wait until he was back in his room and could tell me what was going on himself? What if he never told me? Was there anybody in the entire world I could count on to just tell me the truth?

The one person I'd always counted on was Gram. But she knew even less than I did right now. She didn't know

Joe was in the hospital or that I was in Iowa or that Sam and Suzanne had come back into our lives.

Well, it wasn't my idea to keep all that from her.

Joe wouldn't be happy, but I didn't know what else to do. I couldn't talk to him. And I had to talk to someone. So I picked up the phone and called Gram.

Chapter Thirteen

Why didn't anyone tell me Joe was in the hospital?" Gram asked. She sounded like a little girl. *Why didn't anyone tell* me *I had a mom and sister out there?*

"Joe didn't want you to worry," I said.

"I was worried anyway. I knew something was wrong when he didn't come to visit. He hasn't been to see me in months."

"It hasn't been months," I told her. "The accident was just on Monday. He visited you every day until then."

Gram didn't freak out on me. I had to repeat some things a couple times, but I was pretty sure she understood everything I said about Joe's accident. In fact, she almost seemed like the old Gram. Strong and ready to solve this problem. She said she would call the hospital and see what she could find out about the tests. Then she asked who was taking care of me while Joe was in the hospital...which was exactly the opening I needed to tell her everything else.

I let the whole story pour out—from Sam showing up on our doorstep three weeks ago, to meeting Suzanne for the first time at the police station, to the custody hearing with the judge, to the letter Suzanne wrote me, to my trip here. It felt good to finally tell her. But she was really quiet when I finished.

"Gram? Did you hear everything I just said?"

Did she understand? It took a long time to go through all that. Gram doesn't do well with stories that take a long time to tell.

"Yes, I heard you," Gram said. Her voice sounded different. Far away.

"So…you knew I had a mom and sister out there this whole time."

There was a pause. Then I heard a faint "Yes."

"Why didn't you ever tell me?"

Silence.

"I suppose Joe probably told you not to," I said. "And you probably didn't want to screw things up for him and me."

"I always told him this would come back to haunt him one day," Gram said. "I always told him—" She broke off there. "I-I'm sorry, honey, I can't talk about this today. I need to—"

"Wait!" I cried. "Don't hang up yet! There's something else I need to ask you. And it's not about my mom or Sam."

There was no easy way to bring it up, so I just asked straight out. "Did Joe have a sister?"

Gram didn't respond at first, but I knew she was still

there. I could hear her breathing on the line. Finally, she said, "Someone told you about Katie." It wasn't a question the way she said it.

I heard a door open upstairs. I was going to have to finish this up quick.

"They didn't tell me much," I said. "All they said was Joe used to have a sister and her name was Katie." I heard footsteps on the stairs, so I turned and faced the other direction. "They didn't tell me what happened to her."

"She died. A long time ago."

Yeah, I knew that already. But I had to be careful I didn't push too hard too fast. "Why didn't you or Joe ever talk about her? Grandpa Wright died, too, but you and Joe talked about him."

"That's because he died of cancer."

I didn't get it. Why was it okay to talk about Grandpa Wright, who died of cancer, but it wasn't okay to talk about Katie?

"How did Katie die?" I asked, even though I could hear Sam coming into the room.

"Joe's the one who should be telling you this, not me," Gram said.

"Joe's not here to tell me." *Please, Gram. Please tell me!*

"Or maybe Suzanne," Gram said.

I stared at the phone in my hand. Was she kidding? "You'd rather Suzanne tell me what happened to Joe's sister than tell me yourself?"

Gram took a breath. "Katie...got hit by a car. Your other grandfather...Suzanne's dad...was driving the car that hit her."

"What?" *No way.*

"I can't talk anymore—"

"Wait, Gram! You can't hang up now."

But she already had.

I turned and saw Sam standing right behind me. Her hair was rumpled and messy, but for once she didn't seem to care about her appearance.

"What did you find out?" she asked.

There was no reason to keep it a secret, so I told her what Gram had told me.

"No way," she said as she flounced down on the couch beside me. It was exactly what I'd thought.

"Grandpa Sperling is a really careful driver," Sam went on. "He could never have killed anyone."

"Not intentionally, maybe," I said quietly. "But anyone can have an accident."

Sam shook her head. "You said your grandma had a stroke or something. Maybe she got the story mixed up."

"I don't think so." Gram had sounded more "there" today than she had in a long time.

"Then maybe she just made it up?" Sam put her feet up on the coffee table. "I bet your grandma doesn't like my mom and my grandparents any more than my mom and my grandparents like her."

Suzanne and Grandma and Grandpa Sperling didn't like Gram? Big surprise. "Well, if *your* grandpa killed her daughter, that would make sense." It also explained why Joe and Gram had kept Katie a secret from me. They couldn't have told me my Grandpa Sperling killed her without admitting I actually *had* a Grandpa Sperling.

Would I ever know the whole truth about my life and my family?

Sam looked at me. "There's an easy way to find out whether that's what happened or not."

I didn't see why she refused to believe it.

"We can look it up online," she said, sitting back up. "Right now. Mom already packed our computer, but we could go to the library. Something like that would've been in the newspaper, don't you think?"

I shrugged. "Probably. But aren't you supposed to finish packing your stuff before we go anywhere?"

She tucked her hair behind her ear. "Don't you think this is a little more important than packing? Let me get dressed and then we can go."

Whatever. It wasn't my room.

I have to say Sam was dressed and ready to go in record time for her. She came back in about fifteen minutes wearing blue shorts and a T-shirt. Her hair was combed and she even had a little makeup on. "Ready?" she asked, putting her purse on her shoulder.

"Sure." I gave Sherlock a pat good-bye, then followed Sam out to the garage.

She pressed a button and the garage door went up. "You can ride my mom's bike," she said, nodding toward a red and silver bike in the corner.

Bike?

"Uh, Sam?" I said as she wheeled the other bike toward the open garage door. "I don't know how to ride a bike."

Sam stopped. "You're kidding."

"No." I definitely was *not* kidding. Bikes cost money. Plus we haven't lived a lot of places where you could ride a bike.

"I know how to drive a car, though." Not that that helped us any right now. There wasn't one here to drive.

Sam rolled her eyes. "Right. You can't ride a bike, but you can drive a car."

I probably shouldn't have told her that, but I didn't want her to think I was an idiot just because I couldn't ride a bike. "Look, don't tell your mom," I said. "But Joe taught me to drive when I was ten." Eleven, actually. Because when I thought I was ten, I was really eleven.

Sam leaned against her bike. "You really know how to drive?"

"Lots of farm kids learn how to drive when they're really young," I said. Not that I was ever a farm kid. But that was what Joe had told me. He said he'd learned to drive when he was ten.

"Wow," Sam said. "That's so cool. I've never even sat in the driver's seat of a car."

I remembered the first time I sat in the driver's seat. I was a little scared, but Joe told me to relax. To think of the wheel as an extension of my arms and the pedals as an extension of my feet. He said driving wasn't any more complicated than walking. And it wasn't. It was amazing. I felt like I was flying every time I did it. Not that I got to do it a lot.

"Well, I don't know how we're going to get to the library if you don't know how to ride a bike," Sam said glumly. "It's like two miles to the library from here."

"Two miles?" That was nothing. "Can't we walk?"

"Walk?" Sam gaped at me.

"Yeah. It only takes half an hour to walk two miles. Forty-five minutes tops."

"I guess," Sam said. "I don't know how else we're going to get there."

* * *

The library was a small brick building on the edge of downtown. We went in and immediately headed for the row of computers. It turned out the *Clearwater Gazette* had all their newspapers online. Even the ones from back when our parents were kids. And they were searchable. Sam typed Katie's name in the box. Several articles came up.

Sam clicked on the top one. "Here we go," she said, squinting at the screen.

Gram was right. According to the article, Katie Wright, age twelve, had been riding her bike home from school when she was hit by a car on Rosewood Avenue. The driver of the vehicle was Samuel Sperling, age fifty-five. The twelve-year-old unexpectedly swerved into the path of Mr. Sperling's vehicle. Katie Wright died at the scene. Mr. Sperling was not charged.

For a while, Sam and I just stared at the screen. Neither of us said a word.

"How come nobody ever told me about this?" Sam asked in a small voice.

"No one ever told me, either," I reminded her.

Sam scrolled back to the beginning of the article, then all the way to the top of that day's news. "Look at the date on here. Mom would've only been fourteen when this happened. This was before our parents even got together."

"I'm surprised they ever did get together," I said. "*Their* parents couldn't have been very happy about it."

"My grandma always said the two of them should never have gotten married," Sam said. "I always thought she meant they were just so different. But if Grandpa Sperling…" She couldn't even say the words.

"Their marriage was doomed right from the start," I said.

We logged off the computer and left the library. We wandered around downtown for a while, each lost in our own thoughts. If this was *The Parent Trap*, we would've been trying to figure out a way to get our parents back together quick before Suzanne married Bob. But I think we both realized how hopeless that was. Even before I knew about Katie, I couldn't imagine Joe with someone like Suzanne at all. She was obsessed with rules. Joe hardly paid any attention to rules.

Eventually we got hungry and wandered into a diner called The Redhead, which was kind of a funky place. None of the tables matched. Each one was painted bright red or yellow or blue or green. The menu was written on a chalkboard at the front of the restaurant and water was served in glass jars like the ones in Gram's basement that were filled with green beans or pickles.

Sam and I both ordered the grown-up grilled cheese sandwich, then we sat back and waited for our food to come. I wondered what was going through Sam's head. She was the one who'd started this whole thing when she went searching for her dad. She was the one who'd wanted to know the truth about what happened all those years ago. Did she ever, for just one second, wish she hadn't found anything?

"Are you going to tell your mom and your grandparents that we know about Katie?" I asked Sam.

"I'll tell my mom. Eventually. What about you? Are you going to tell Joe?"

Joe had kept all kinds of secrets from me, but I'd never kept one from him before. I'd also never done something he specifically told me not to do before. Not until earlier this morning when I called Gram and told her all the things Joe didn't want me to tell her.

"I don't know," I said. Thinking about Joe right now reminded me I'd never called back to see what the deal was with those tests yesterday. But I couldn't sneak away to make a call now. The waitress was coming with our food.

"So what's Grandma Wright like?" Sam asked as she put her napkin in her lap. "Is she like Grandma Sperling? Or is she more like Bob's mother?"

"Neither," I said, picking up my sandwich. How did someone describe Gram? "She's not as uptight as your Grandma Sperling...and she's not as bubbly as Bob's mother. She's just...Gram. She's strong and smart, at least she was before her stroke." I never would've guessed she'd had a kid who died. She'd never seemed sad or depressed.

I took another bite of my sandwich. It was made with fancier bread and stronger-tasting cheese than I was used to, but I liked it. There was something weird about the fries, though. I couldn't decide whether I liked them or not.

"What's the deal with these?" I asked, holding one out to Sam. They were a different color than most fries. More orange.

"They're sweet potato fries," Sam replied.

"Sweet potato fries?" I dropped the fry onto my plate. "I don't like sweet potatoes."

"I don't like them, either," Sam said, popping a fry into her mouth. "I hate that marshmallow stuff people put on them at Thanksgiving. But they're okay as fries."

"Really?" I picked up another fry and nibbled on it. Maybe I could get used to them. Gram always said you could get used to anything if you tried.

The waitress cleared our plates after we were done eating, but neither Sam nor I made any move to leave.

"Do you actually remember when Joe and I lived with you and your mom?" I asked.

Sam picked up the saltshaker and turned it around in her hand. "A little," she said. "It's mostly just bits and pieces."

"Like what?"

"I don't know. Playing Barbies."

"Barbies!" I croaked. "I've never had a Barbie doll."

Sam laughed. "We had all kinds of Barbies and Barbie stuff. It's still in our basement."

"It's probably all yours. I never played Barbies."

"Yes, you did," Sam insisted. "We played Barbies together. With Mom. That's something I remember."

I didn't believe it. "I was only three when I..." What would you call it? What did I do? "When I went to live with

Joe," I decided. "You don't give a Barbie doll to a three-year-old. They could choke on all that crap Barbie wears. The shoes and purses and whatever."

Sam's smile grew wider. "I'm telling you, you played Barbies."

The weird thing was I was starting to see a picture of it in my head. Sam and me playing with a Barbie tent and camper. Setting all our Barbie dolls around a makeshift campfire.

No, I would never have played Barbies. *Would I?*

"Did we have a Barbie camper?" I asked. "Yellow with—"

"Pink decals," we said together.

How could she remember this stuff right off the top of her head? I had to really work at it.

"What else do you remember?" I asked.

"Nothing." Sam put the saltshaker back.

"Nothing? Please tell me you remember something else about me besides playing Barbies."

"Well." Sam lowered her eyes. "I remember when you died."

I shivered. "You do?"

"Again, just bits and pieces," she said.

"Tell me," I said, leaning forward. "What do you remember? Do you remember the day I…disappeared?"

Sam paused for a second. "I remember when Joe came to pick us up. It was the last memory I had of him before this year."

She had almost no memories of Joe. And I had almost no memories of Suzanne.

"It was the last time he was going to see us for a while," Sam said, "because you and I were going to move to Florida with Mom so she could go to medical school. We were all going to live with Grandma and Grandpa Sperling and they were going to take care of us while Mom was in school. But I was sick that day, so Mom wouldn't let me go with you and Joe. They had this huge fight because it was the last time he was going to get to see us and he wanted me to go with you guys, even though I was sick."

"What happened when Joe came back without me?" I asked.

"He didn't come back."

"He didn't?"

"No. When you guys left, that was the last time he was ever at our house. And it was the last time I ever saw you." She sounded so sad when she said that. Like she really lost something that day. Which I guess she did. She lost her sister. Her twin sister.

But what about me? I lost my sister, too. The only difference is I never knew I lost anything. *Why didn't I remember her the way she remembered me?* How could two people have such different memories?

"I think you and I should make a pact," Sam said suddenly. "Right now."

"What kind of pact?"

"From now on, no matter what happens between us or our parents or anyone else, we should always tell each other the truth. About everything. Okay?" She looked at me expectantly.

It was a nice idea. And right that second I felt closer to

her than I'd ever felt before. Maybe even closer than I'd ever felt to anyone. After everything we'd been through, I liked the idea of Sam and me always telling each other the truth.

But I couldn't tell her the whole truth. Not about everything. Not about Joe being in the hospital. If Suzanne and the Sperlings found out, they wouldn't let me go back to him.

"You don't want to make a pact?" she asked when I didn't answer right away.

"No, I do," I said. "From now on, we tell each other the truth." I even held out my right hand over the table so we could shake.

But I crossed my fingers on the hand in my lap.

Chapter Fourteen

They're back, Suzanne!" Grandma Sperling called up the stairs as soon as Sam and I walked in the front door. She and Grandpa Sperling were all dressed up and ready to go to the rehearsal.

Footsteps pounded down the stairs. "Where have you girls been?" Suzanne asked as she strode barefoot into the room. Her white blouse hung loosely over her dark blue skirt. "I told you girls to be home at three. It's almost three thirty."

"Apparently Sarah was never taught to respect the clock," Grandma Sperling said as she adjusted Grandpa Sperling's tie.

"It wasn't T.J.'s fault," Sam spoke up right away. "We were talking and—"

"Regardless of what you were doing, Samantha," Grandma Sperling said, her back to me, "*you* know what's expected of you."

I was getting awfully tired of Grandma Sperling's attitude toward me. "Are you saying I *don't* know what's expected of me?" I asked.

"No one's saying anything of the sort," Suzanne said with a pointed look at Grandma Sperling. "Now you girls really need to start getting ready—" She tried to lead Sam and me toward the stairs, but I pulled away.

"Why don't you just say what you're thinking. Say it to my face," I told Grandma Sperling. It was time she and I had it out once and for all. "You think Joe is a bad father, don't you?"

Grandma Sperling didn't say it, but we all knew she thought it.

"I know he made a mistake when he took me," I went on. "But it's not like he's the only one who made mistakes." I could feel Sam tense up beside me. "Sam and I know about the mistake *he* made." I waved my hand at Grandpa Sperling. "We know he killed my dad's sister!"

Grandpa Sperling sank to the couch and closed his eyes. All the color drained from his face.

"That is hardly comparable to what your father did," Grandma Sperling said in a tight voice.

"Are you kidding? Look at me!" I spread my arms out. "I'm *alive!* But Joe's sister isn't. How is what your husband did any better than what Joe did?"

"It isn't," Grandpa Sperling murmured.

"What are you talking about?" Grandma Sperling asked as she whirled to face Grandpa Sperling. "You never meant to hit that girl. What happened that day was a terrible accident. But Joseph *meant* to take Sarah. He—"

Grandpa Sperling held up one hand. "It doesn't matter. Do you think that poor girl's mother cared whether it was an accident or not? She lost her child, just like Suzanne lost her child."

"It's not the same," Grandma Sperling insisted. "Joseph Wright was a—"

"STOP!" Suzanne yelled. "I don't want to talk about this! I don't want to talk about what Joe did and I don't want to talk about what Dad did. I'm getting married tomorrow. This is supposed to be a happy time for me. Can we please just be happy right now?"

Grandma Sperling tried to smile. "Of course, dear," she said, backing down. "You've been through so much." She shot me a dirty look, like it was my fault Suzanne wasn't happy. "Now why don't you girls go upstairs and get ready for the rehearsal dinner?"

Sam and I glanced at each other as we turned and headed up the stairs. But neither of us said a word. I went into the den and Sam continued down the hall to her room. Was she mad at me for bringing all that stuff up? Well, even if she was, I didn't regret it one bit.

I liked Grandpa Sperling. I really did. I liked that he played the tuba and I liked that he liked my dog and I even liked his lame magic tricks. But I'm sorry, what he did *was* worse than what Joe did. He *killed* someone.

But wait a second. Suzanne and Sam and everyone else back here believed I was dead all these years, too.

Was what Grandpa Sperling did really any worse than what Joe did?

No. Stop. I didn't want to think about this anymore,

either. I needed to talk to Joe. I pulled Sam's cell phone out of my front pocket, flipped it open, and punched in the number for Joe's hospital room. My heart went thump, thump, thump while I waited for someone, *anyone,* to pick up the phone.

No one did.

Unfortunately, I couldn't just sit here and keep calling the hospital. I had to get ready for this wedding rehearsal. I took off my tennis shoes and put on my black pants and white shirt. Uh-oh. I suddenly realized those tennis shoes were the only shoes I had. Even *I* knew you didn't wear tennis shoes with dress pants. The pink shoes that Suzanne bought to go with my last-minute bridesmaid dress probably wouldn't work, either.

What was I going to do?

Maybe Sam had something I could borrow? I really didn't want to have another run-in with Suzanne or Grandma Sperling. I cracked my door open just a little bit and checked the hallway. The coast was clear, so I crept down to Sam's room and knocked softly on her door.

"Yeah?" she said, flinging her door open. She had changed into a black skirt and black-and-white blouse. "Hey, nice pants!"

"Thanks," I said, even though they were just regular old dress pants. "I forgot to pack shoes for this outfit. Do you have some I could borrow?"

"Sure, come on in." She grabbed my arm and pulled me into her room. "Most of my shoes are packed, but we can unpack them," she said. She went to the stack of boxes by her window, moved the top one to the floor, then put the next one on her bed. She opened it up and I saw that the whole box was full of shoes.

"Holy cow!" I said. "Are these *all* yours?"

She smiled as she pulled out black shoe after black shoe after black shoe and lined up all the pairs on her bed. She didn't even seem embarrassed about having so many. "Do you want to wear shoes or sandals?" she asked. She had several pairs of each.

"Doesn't matter," I said.

She grabbed a pair of sandals that had at least two-inch heels. "These are nice. And they kind of look like the ones I'm planning to wear. See?" She pointed to another pair of black sandals that lay in front of her dresser. Both pairs looked extremely uncomfortable.

"Could I maybe wear those?" I pointed at a pair of plain black flat-soled shoes on her bed.

"Those don't have heels."

"Yeah. I know." That was why I'd picked them.

"Don't you like heels?" she asked.

"Not exactly." Why would anyone like heels?

She shrugged and picked up her curling iron. "You can wear them if you want."

"Thanks," I said, slipping them on. They weren't too bad for dress shoes.

"So. Pretty intense scene down there, huh?" I said.

"Yeah," she said as she twirled a section of hair around the hot curling iron.

"Are you mad at me for bringing that up about your grandpa?" I asked.

"He's your grandpa, too," she said. She squeezed open

her curling iron and a perfect corkscrew curl dropped to her shoulder. "And no, I'm not mad. Now everyone knows that we know and hopefully there won't be any more secrets. There've been way too many of them in this family. And way too many things that people don't want to talk about."

"Yeah, I—"

"Wait!" Grandma Sperling yelled from downstairs. "Come back here, dog. Here, doggie, doggie!"

What the—? There was only one dog in this house. I flew down the stairs to see what was going on. I found Grandma Sperling standing in the open front door still calling, "Here, doggie, doggie!"

"Did you let Sherlock out?" I cried. I brushed past her and caught a glimpse of white disappearing behind a bush at the end of the block. "Is that my dog down there?"

"I-I didn't mean to—," Grandma Sperling stammered, wringing her hands. "I just opened the door and—"

"Why would you do that?" I yelled. But I didn't have time to stand there. I had to get my dog.

"Sherlock! Sherlock, come!" I screamed as I raced down the street, my eyes peeled on that row of bushes up ahead.

It was hard to run in Sam's dress shoes, so I kicked them off and nudged them to the edge of the sidewalk. Then I took off running again. The concrete burned the bottoms of my feet, but it was better than running in those shoes. When I got to the bushes, I searched all around, but I didn't see my dog.

I cupped my hands around my mouth and yelled, "Sherlock!"

The lady who lived in the house by the bushes opened her door. She was older than Suzanne, but not as old as Grandma Sperling. She didn't look too happy to see me standing in her front yard.

"Did you see a white dog?" I asked her. "He was just here, under this bush."

The lady scowled at me. "You shouldn't let your dog run loose."

"Hey, I'm not the one who let him out!" I called as I ran around behind her house. I didn't see him, but I heard him bark.

"Sherlock?" I called. It sounded like he had cut through the yard behind this one and was on the next street. I followed the sound of his bark, but when I got over to the other front yard, I still didn't see him.

I kept running and calling, "Sherlock! Where are you, boy?"

I darted across a street, my eyes scanning both directions, and then I saw him. He was about a block and a half away, scampering across the yards.

I rested my hands against my thighs, my chest heaving. "Stop, Sherlock!" I panted.

He barked again, then turned and ran away. Great. He thought we were playing a game. But this wasn't a game. He was heading for the highway.

"SHERLOCK!" I screamed, running harder than I'd ever run in my life.

He ran past the last house on the block. There was just a grassy hill separating him from the divided highway now. The highway we'd driven into town on. I chased him up the hill, but I couldn't see him once he started down the other side.

I heard a car honk and the squeal of brakes.

"NO!!!" I was so scared I was going to find my dog splayed out all over the road, but when I got to the top of the hill…no Sherlock. And no stopped cars.

So where was my dog now? There was a field of some sort across the highway. Beans, I think. Was he in the bean field? I waited for a gap in traffic, then scurried across the highway. Ouch! The road was even hotter than the sidewalk.

"Sherlock!" I called, running along the edge of the field. "Where are you, boy?" I peered down each row as I passed it.

Finally, I caught a blur of white. I backed up and there was my dog, plowing down that row as fast as his little legs could carry him. I tore after him, mud oozing up between my toes. He saw me coming and tried to plunge through the bean plants, but they were too thick. He couldn't get through.

"I've almost got you!" I told him. I could tell he was looking for another gap between the plants. But before he could worm his whole body through, I made a grab for him. "Ha! Got you!" I cried, picking him up and squeezing him tight against my shirt.

Uh-oh. My white shirt wasn't so white anymore. My black pants were caked with mud. And my feet looked like…well, like I'd just run barefoot through a bean field.

I checked my watch. It was 4:30. We were supposed to be at the church for Suzanne's wedding rehearsal at 5:00. I wasn't even sure how to get back to Suzanne's from here. Even if I did manage to get back before they left, I was in no shape to go to a wedding rehearsal and fancy dinner. Well, it was Grandma Sperling's fault for letting Sherlock out. Had she let him out on purpose? Or was it an accident? Either way, he could have been *killed*.

Holding my dirty dog tight, I turned around and made my way out of the field. I didn't dare put him down because I didn't have his leash. I wasn't going to give him another chance to run away. I shifted his weight in my arms so it was easier to carry him, then walked back along the dirt shoulder of the highway. I hadn't been walking very long before I saw a familiar dark blue Honda slow and pull over on the other side of the highway.

Suzanne.

The driver's window lowered and Suzanne stuck her head out. "T.J. Over here," she called. She was alone.

I looked both ways, then ran barefoot across the hot paved highway. "I don't think you want us to ride in your car," I told Suzanne. "We're both pretty muddy."

"I know you are," she said. "It's fine. Just get in."

Okay. I set Sherlock on the floor of the backseat and told him to stay. Then I crawled in and tried to take up as little space as possible. "Thank you for picking us up," I said as she pulled out onto the highway. She was supposed to be at her wedding rehearsal, after all. Not driving around looking for me.

"I'm glad you found your dog," Suzanne said, watching me in the rearview mirror. "I'm sorry he got out."

She was sorry? What about Grandma Sperling?

"You know, your dad used to have a dog that looked a lot like your Sherlock."

"I know. He told me."

"Did he also tell you that that dog was the reason we got together?"

My head popped up. "No."

"It's true," Suzanne said, slowing for a stoplight. "It was about a year after Joe's sister was killed. I was walking home from school and this dog came out of nowhere. I saw your dad running down the block after him. He yelled for me to help him. So I did."

I tried to picture a teenaged Joe and Suzanne chasing after a dog that looked like Sherlock, but I just couldn't see it.

"Did you know who he was?"

"You mean, did I know he was the boy whose sister was killed in an accident because of my dad?" she asked. The light turned green and we kept going. "Yes, I knew. I'd never actually spoken him before, but I knew who he was. And I felt guilty every time I saw him in the halls. Like somehow what happened was my fault, even though I wasn't even in the car.

"But we had a really nice talk that afternoon," Suzanne went on. "After we caught his dog, I mean. We talked for a long time and I realized we had something pretty big in common."

"Really?" I said. "What?" I'd known Suzanne for two days now and I couldn't think of a single thing she and Joe had in common.

"We both had families that were consumed with grief."

"That's why you guys got together?"

"Initially, yes," Suzanne said. "But in the end, it's probably what broke us up, too. That, and the fact that the shared grief was about the only thing Joe and I did have in common. You can't build a relationship on grief."

No, I guess not.

Suzanne and I didn't talk anymore until we were back on her street. "I, um, left Sam's shoes in the grass over there," I said as we drove past them.

Suzanne slowed the car and pulled over. I jumped out and got the shoes. "I can just walk the rest of the way back to your house," I said. But Suzanne motioned for me to get back in the car, so...I did.

"I know this is a difficult time for you, T.J.," Suzanne said. "It's difficult for all of us. But we're going to find a way to make this work. You just have to give it some time, okay? Please. Give us all some time."

"Okay," I said.

As though it was really that easy.

Chapter Fifteen

Grandma Sperling met Suzanne and me at the front door when we walked in. I carried my muddy, wiggly dog in my arms.

"It's five after five," she told Suzanne. "We were supposed to be at the church five minutes ago!"

"I know, Mother," Suzanne said, stepping around her. Grandpa Sperling and Sam were on the couch, all dressed up and ready to go.

"Good heavens," Grandma Sperling cried. "Look at you, Sar—T.J. You're a mess."

I blinked. Did she just call me T.J.? "I-I had to chase Sherlock through a field," I said as I set him down. He ran right over to Sam and she scratched him behind the ears.

"It's fine, Mother," Suzanne said. "I'm going to call Bob right now. T.J. is going to go and get changed and then we'll be on our way."

I am? "Uh, what do you want me to wear?" I called after her as she dashed into the kitchen. "I didn't exactly bring any other dressy clothes."

"Just put on something clean," she called back. "It doesn't have to be dressy. And hurry up!"

I pounded up the stairs two at a time, stopped in the bathroom long enough to wash my hands, arms, and feet, then I hurried back to the den. Sam's cat was curled up on my bed. He meowed at me like he was telling me to hurry up.

"I'm going as fast as I can," I told him. It was too hot for jeans, so I grabbed a clean pair of shorts and a red shirt and threw them on. I also grabbed Sam's cell phone in case I had a chance to call Joe later. I hustled back downstairs, my tennis shoes dangling from my fingers.

Grandma Sperling gasped when she saw me. "You can't go to the church dressed like that!"

"She's fine, Mother," Suzanne said. "It's just the rehearsal. Let's go."

When we got to the church, Suzanne and Grandma Sperling rushed us all inside. I'd only been inside a church two or three times in my whole life but I didn't exactly have a chance to look around. We went right into the main part of the church, where everyone was waiting.

Bob and a bunch of other people were sitting in the first two pews on the right side. The minister stood beside them.

"Sorry we're late," Suzanne said as we practically ran up the aisle. "We had a dog emergency."

Bob stood up and greeted Suzanne with a hug. "I was afraid you'd changed your mind about this wedding," he said.

Suzanne smiled. "You know better than that."

I recognized most of the people who were there from

last night's barbecue. Apparently Bob's brothers and sisters were all in the wedding. But there was one lady I hadn't met before.

Suzanne introduced us. "T.J., I'd like you to meet my oldest friend in the world. This is Paula Wachowski, my matron of honor."

Paula held out her hand. "We've met, but you probably don't remember." She smiled. "I helped take care of you and your sister when you were babies. It's so nice to see you again."

I felt weird when she said that. *So nice to see you again.* She made it sound like we'd just been too busy to see each other these past ten years.

"Let's run through the ceremony now, shall we?" the minister said. All the people who were in the wedding got up and moved toward the aisle between the pews. I was usually pretty comfortable in shorts and a T-shirt, but I felt a little funny today when everyone else was so dressed up.

"Oh, wait," Bob's mother said. "You need your bouquet, Suzanne." She reached into a bag, pulled out a paper plate with a bunch of gift bows on it and handed it to her.

"What the heck?" I said to Sam as Suzanne took the plate and gave Bob's mother a hug.

"They made it at Mom's bridal shower," Sam told me. "The bows came from all the presents she got."

"Okay," I said. "So why'd they put them all on a paper plate?"

Sam shrugged. "It's just something they do in that family before people get married. I don't know. Maybe it's supposed to bring good luck or something."

"How do you want everyone to line up?" the minister asked Suzanne and Bob.

"They've added a bridesmaid," Grandma Sperling said as she squeezed in next to the minister. "So I don't know what they're going to do about that. Somebody's not going to have anyone to walk with."

"We've had other weddings where the number of bridesmaids and the number of groomsmen didn't match up," the minister said. "I remember one wedding where the groomsmen walked in with the groom and then stood at the front of the church with him while the bridesmaids walked up the aisle by themselves."

"That would work," Paula said, turning to Suzanne.

"You're still going to have an uneven number of people standing at the front of the church," Grandma Sperling said. "It's going to look off balance."

"Hey, if it's a problem, I don't have to be a bridesmaid," I said. I didn't want to be responsible for making Suzanne's wedding look off balance.

"No, I should be the person who backs out," one of Bob's sisters said. "In fact, T.J. looks about my size. She could probably wear my bridesmaid dress if you'd rather everyone matches."

Then all that shopping would have been for nothing.

"Nonsense," Bob's mother said. "Neither one of you should back out."

"That's right," Suzanne said. "I asked you both to be in my wedding because I wanted you both there. I like the idea of the bridesmaids walking in by themselves. What do you think, dear?" she asked Bob.

"I think that would work," he said. I had a feeling Bob didn't care either way.

"And I don't think it matters if there's an uneven number of bridesmaids and groomsmen standing at the front of the church," Suzanne added. Grandma Sperling sort of scowled.

"Well, let's try it, then," the minister said. "Bridesmaids, why don't you go with Suzanne. Line up in the order you're going to be in tomorrow. Bob, groomsmen, come with me."

All the men who were in the wedding walked through a door at the front of the church. Suzanne, Grandpa Sperling, and all the bridesmaids moved to the back of the church. Grandma Sperling trotted after the bridesmaids. Everyone else sat in the pews and watched us. "What order do we walk in?" Sam asked.

"Well, your mom goes last," one of Bob's sisters said. "She's the bride. And Paula goes second to the last since she's the matron of honor. The rest of us? I don't know. It's up to you, Suzanne."

"The girls should go first," Grandma Sperling said.

"Okay. But which of us goes *first* first?" Sam asked.

"You do," I said. That way I could watch her and do whatever she did.

"I think they should go together," Paula said.

"Oh, I like that idea," Suzanne said. So Sam and I moved to the front of the line and stood side by side.

"Are you all ready back there?" the minister called from the front of the church.

"Ready," Suzanne said. She held her paper plate bouquet in front of her like it was a real bouquet of flowers and smiled. Grandpa Sperling stood quietly beside her.

"Ready," Sam called back to the minister.

"Okay, you two start walking as soon as the music starts," the minister told Sam and me. He nodded to someone in the balcony and a couple of violins started playing. Whoa. I wasn't expecting violin music. And I wasn't expecting to hear a song that wasn't "Here Comes the Bride." Wasn't that the official wedding song?

I watched as Bob, the minister, and the four groomsmen strode out of that little side room at the front of the church. They looked like soldiers. The minister and the groomsmen marched up the steps, but Bob went and stood down by the front pew.

"Come on," Sam hissed, grabbing my arm. "The music started."

"Remember, girls," the minister said over the violins. "This is a solemn occasion. Walk with the music. And with each other."

We *were* walking with each other.

Right foot. Left foot. Right foot. Left foot. I felt really stupid because everyone was watching us. I hoped we were doing it right. I also felt stupid because I was wearing shorts and a T-shirt while Sam was wearing this pretty skirt and blouse. We didn't match and for once I sort of wished we did.

"Where do we go?" I asked Sam as we approached the end of the aisle.

"I think we go up the stairs and stand on the other side from where the guys are standing."

"That's right," the minister said. "Go all the way down so you leave room for the other bridesmaids."

When we got there I wasn't sure which direction we were supposed to face: the front of the church or the back. The groomsmen were all facing the back, so Sam and I turned around, too. By then one of Bob's sisters was already on the steps, the other was halfway up the aisle, and Paula was just starting down the aisle.

Once all the bridesmaids got to the front of the church, the music stopped. But Suzanne and Grandpa Sperling were still back where we started. What was going on? Why did the music stop and why were Suzanne and her father just standing there?

"All rise," the minister said and the few people who were in the pews stood up.

A trumpet and piano started to play. I didn't know what they were playing, but it gave me goose bumps because it sounded so majestic. You'd think the president of the United States was coming into the church, but it was just Suzanne, clutching her paper plate bouquet with one hand and Grandpa Sperling's elbow with the other. *This is my mother,* I thought. *She looks so…beautiful.*

Sam nudged me. "What's the matter?" she whispered. "You look like you're going to cry or something."

What? I did not. "I never cry," I informed her.

"You look like you're going to."

I sniffed. "Well, I'm not."

And I didn't.

162

After that the minister went through the whole service and explained what happened when. The singers ran through their song, which was some lovey-dovey thing I'd never heard before. Then the minister explained how the unity candle worked and where everyone was supposed to stand when it was being lit. While he was talking, Sam's cell phone rang inside my front pocket.

Everyone, including the minister, looked toward me and Sam.

"Samantha!" Suzanne cried. "You know better than to bring your cell phone to church."

"She didn't bring it," I said as I slid the phone out of my pocket. It rang even louder then. "I brought it." But whoever was calling obviously wasn't calling me; they were calling Sam. And since it wasn't my phone, I didn't know how to make it stop ringing.

Sam grabbed her phone out of my hand and turned it off. Then she looked around for a place to stash it. "I'll put it back in my pocket," I told her.

"No," Grandma Sperling said. "*I'll* take it." She marched up the steps us with her hand outstretched. This time she gave us both a nasty look.

Sam had no choice but to hand the phone over to her grandmother.

No! How was I going to call Joe now?

After the rehearsal we went to this really fancy restaurant for dinner. All the tables had white tablecloths and candles in little bowls. And was that steak that I smelled back in the kitchen? I still felt out of place in my shorts. Not to mention cold. The air conditioning must have been cranked all the way up. But once we sat down, no one could see my shorts anymore. I sat at a table with Sam and Suzanne and Bob. Grandma and Grandpa Sperling sat at another table with Bob's parents.

It *was* steak that I smelled. Once everyone was seated, the waiters started bringing out plates and setting them in front of people. I love steak, but I haven't had it very often. When I got my plate, I just leaned over and breathed in the smell. There was also a weird green vegetable that came in long spears. I wasn't sure what that was. And mashed potatoes with the peels mixed in. Mmm… I couldn't wait to dig in.

I picked up my knife and started cutting. My knife slid through the meat like it was soft butter. I popped a piece into my mouth and just about died, it tasted so good. Then I realized I was the only one eating. In fact, I was the only one who'd even started cutting the steak. I slowly set down my silverware. What was the deal? We all had this amazing meal in front of us. Why wasn't anyone eating it?

"Go ahead," Bob said to me and everyone else at the table. "Eat."

Sam and I glanced at each other out of the corners of our eyes, then we both started eating. Once I started, I couldn't stop. Not until I'd cleaned my whole plate. Man, that was one of the best meals I'd ever had. In fact, it was so good I felt a little bit guilty. Joe sure wasn't having a meal like this in the hospital.

I leaned over to Sam and whispered, "Do you think you can get your phone back from your grandma?"

She didn't look real thrilled about trying. "I don't know," she whispered back. "Maybe. Why?"

"I want to call Joe." Everyone else was still eating and talking and laughing, so this seemed like a good time to sneak out and try to make a phone call.

She looked confused. "But we already know about Katie."

"I know. I just want to talk to him." Joe and I still had a lot to talk about.

Sam wiped her mouth with her napkin, then got up and made her way over to the grandparent table. I watched as she put her head close to Grandma Sperling's, but I couldn't tell whether her grandmother was going to give her the phone or not.

Yes! Grandma Sperling leaned over and pulled Sam's phone out of her purse. When Sam came back, she slipped the phone into my hand.

"Thanks," I said.

I started to stand up and Suzanne asked, "Where are you going, T.J.?"

Uh-oh. Could she see the phone? I put that hand behind my back and said, "I need to go to the bathroom. I'll be right back."

She wasn't going to make Sam come with me, was she?

"Don't be too long," she said. "There'll be dessert in a little bit."

"Okay," I said. I meandered around all the tables and through the restaurant lobby. When I went out the door a blast of warm air hit me.

I opened Sam's phone and punched in the number for Joe's hospital room. Once again, nobody answered. I sighed as I slammed Sam's phone shut.

Why wasn't Joe answering his phone?

* * *

The next morning everyone was bustling around the house like crazy. Suzanne was trying to get ready for the wedding, trying to pack her overnight bag for the hotel that night, and trying to make sure she didn't forget anything. Grandma Sperling had made bacon and eggs and was trying to get everyone to sit down and eat, but Grandpa Sperling was the only one who actually did. I reached for a slice of bacon, then went to see what Sam was doing. She was running around her room gathering up earrings, a bracelet, and a hair clip.

"Hey, do you still have my phone?" she asked when she saw me standing in her doorway.

"Do you need it?" I really didn't want to give it back. Not until I talked to Joe.

She looked at me funny. "Not at the moment. But I should charge it up in case I need it later."

It was her phone. I couldn't think of a reason to keep it if she wanted it back.

"I'll go get it," I said. When I came back she wasn't in her room anymore. She was in the bathroom, messing with her hair.

Suzanne breezed past us, then did a double take when

she saw what Sam was doing. "Sam! Why are you curling your hair? You've got an appointment in half an hour."

"Because I haven't decided what I want them to do with my hair!"

Suzanne sighed. "I thought you were going to have them pin it up."

"I don't know. I might want it long and curly. I'm trying something different."

"Well, are you ready to go?"

"Yes."

"What about you, T.J.?" Suzanne asked. "Are you ready to go?"

"Go? Go where?"

"To the hairdresser's," Suzanne said like I should have known.

"I don't need to go to the hairdresser."

Suzanne took a deep breath. I thought she was going to lose it there for a second, but I honestly wasn't trying to make her mad.

"Look, my hair isn't even an inch long." I pinched a section of my hair to show her. "What do I need to go to a hairdresser for? I can just wash it here. They're not going to comb it any different than I would."

"You don't want to go to the hairdresser with Grandma, Sam, and me?"

"Not really." It seemed like a big waste of money.

"Well, okay," Suzanne said a little reluctantly. "You'll be here by yourself, though. Grandpa's going to come along and get his suit while we're at the hairdressers."

Great! Then I could try Joe again.

I tried not to appear too eager for them to leave. But it had been way too long since I'd talked to Joe and it took them way too long to get going.

Once they were gone, I ran up to Sam's room and looked around for her phone, but I couldn't find it. She must have taken it with her. Suzanne probably had hers with her, too, but I went into her bedroom to check. The room smelled like her. All soapy and flowery. I felt funny being in her room when she wasn't home, and I didn't see her phone, so I left.

I decided there wasn't any reason I couldn't use their main phone. As long as it could make long-distance phone calls. So I went into the kitchen, picked up the phone, and punched in Joe's number at the hospital.

The call went through.

"Hello?" Someone answered this time. A woman. It sounded like the same woman I'd talked to yesterday.

"I'd like to talk to my dad. Joseph Wright."

"I'm sorry. He's not here anymore."

"What do you mean? Where is he?"

"I don't know. All I know is his bed is made up and he's not here." There was a pause and I heard another voice in the background. "My husband says the nurses gathered up his things late yesterday afternoon. We don't know what happened to him."

Chapter Sixteen

I called the main number for the hospital and asked to talk to the nurse on Joe's floor. "I'm sorry," the nurse said. "Your father is no longer a patient here."

"Why not? Where'd he go?" He couldn't possibly have gone home. Not without anyone there to take care of him.

"I'm sorry," she said. "I cannot release that information." It was the same thing they'd told me yesterday.

"Privacy rules again?" I asked.

"Yes."

"Well, he didn't die or anything, did he?" I didn't really think he had, but when she gave me the same old "I'm sorry, but I cannot release that information" line, I started to wonder.

"I'm his *daughter!*" I cried. "You can't even tell me if my dad is alive or not?"

"I'm sorry—"

I hung up. She wasn't sorry at all.

Joe couldn't have died. He just had a broken back. He was getting better. But if he wasn't in the hospital anymore, where was he? I tried calling our number, just in case he had somehow gotten home, but the answering machine picked up.

I sighed. Why, oh why, hadn't I tried harder to get ahold of him yesterday?

Maybe Gram knew something. She'd said she was going to call the hospital yesterday. I called the nursing home and Nurse Kari answered the phone.

"I'm sorry, T.J.," she said. "Your grandma had another stroke early this morning."

My heart stopped. "What?" No. Not Gram on top of Joe.

Was this stroke my fault? Joe told me not to tell her about Sam and Suzanne.

"Is she…?" I couldn't even say the words.

"She's in the hospital," the nurse said. "We've been trying to reach your dad for the last two hours. Do you know where he is?"

I swallowed hard. "Here's the thing. I'm at…my mom's. In Iowa. And Joe…he…had an accident." I ended up telling Kari the whole story, from the moment Joe's boss called to tell me he fell off the roof to the fact that he was no longer a patient at Fairview and I had no idea where he was now.

"Oh, honey," Kari said. "I'm so sorry." She went on to tell me way more about privacy laws than I ever wanted to know, none of it very helpful. Then she said, "Don't worry about your grandma, she's going to be fine. Right now you should concentrate on finding out where your dad is. I'm not going to be able to help you with that, but why don't you have your mom call the hospital? Maybe she can get some information for you."

"Maybe," I said. But there was no way I was going to get Suzanne involved. I'd figure something out on my own. I always did. "So what hospital did you send Gram to?" Would privacy laws prevent Kari from telling me that, too?

"Fairview Southdale," she said.

Great. The same hospital Joe was at. Or used to be at.

I called Fairview back and asked for Eva Wright's room. But of course, Gram didn't answer. Nobody did. And when I called again and asked to talk to a nurse on Gram's floor, all I found out was that Gram was sleeping and she was "stable."

So now what?

My family was having this huge crisis and there wasn't a thing I could do to help. I couldn't talk to my grandma. I didn't know where Joe was or if he was even alive. And if I gave Suzanne any idea that anything was wrong, I'd probably never be allowed to go home.

* * *

I tried to act normal when everyone came back. "Wow, you guys look nice," I said cheerfully. Grandma Sperling didn't look much different from the last time I saw her, but Suzanne and Sam did. Suzanne's hair was all braided up and twisted around her head. Little white flowers poked through the braids. Sam's hair was braided on the sides, but the back hung long and curly.

"Thank you, T.J." Suzanne beamed.

Sam looked at me like, *What's wrong with you?*

What? Wasn't it normal to compliment people when they'd just come back from the hairdresser's?

We gathered up clothes and shoes and bags of who-knows-what and then headed over to the church. Even though we still had almost two hours before the wedding. What were we going to do for two hours?

I don't know what the guys were doing, but the women—at least the women in Suzanne and Bob's families—all crammed into the church nursery to get dressed and do hair and makeup. It was like a big party in there, all these half-dressed women talking and laughing.

"Let's go over there," Sam said, pointing to a quiet corner of the room, away from everyone else. There was even an easel we could sort of hide behind while we put on our dresses.

What would it be like to be part of a big, happy family like this? I wondered as I gazed over the top of the easel at the people on the other side of the room. A family where everybody loved each other and there were no secrets.

What happened with Joe and me would never happen in this family. No one would ever take a kid away for ten years and let the rest of the family think that kid was dead. It just wouldn't happen. And if someone in this family was in the hospital, no one would have to worry about privacy laws because everyone would already be there at the hospital. All the time. They'd always know what was going on.

"T.J.," Sam said, touching my arm. "You're crying!"

"I am not," I said. But when I blinked, my vision blurred.

I touched my finger to my cheek and realized it was wet. I was crying and I didn't even realize it.

Luckily no one on the other side of the room had noticed. I wiped my cheeks and blinked a few times. *What was the matter with me?* Sam reached into her purse and pulled out a small package of tissues, but I shook my head.

"I'm fine," I said.

"You don't look fine. In fact, you didn't look fine when we got back from the hairdresser's. What's wrong?"

"Nothing." I went over to the sink and checked my reflection in the mirror above it. Sam was right; I looked terrible. *Pull it together, T.J. Pull it together!* I turned on the cold water and splashed some on my face.

Sam followed me. I could feel her standing there behind me. "Even though this is 'the happiest day of our mother's life,' it's kind of a sad day, too," she said as she yanked a couple of paper towels out of the dispenser and handed them to me. "For us, I mean."

I took the paper towels and dried my face in them as she went on. "I know our parents are never going to get back together, but there was still a small part of me that hoped maybe they would. You know, after they both got over what Joe did."

Would they ever get over that? "Our parents should never have gotten together in the first place," I said as I tossed the paper towel into the trash.

"No. Probably not," Sam agreed. "Do you want me to put some makeup on your face, so it's not so obvious you've been crying?"

Normally I would've said no. I'd never worn makeup

before and saw no reason to start now. But wasn't that what other girls did before their mom got married? Put on makeup?

* * *

A lot of people had come to see Suzanne and Bob get married. When we lined up to walk down the aisle, the main part of the church was mostly full. It was really quiet in there, except for the piano that was playing classical music. But people were talking softly out where we were.

Bob's mother and Grandma Sperling strolled up and down the line of bridesmaids, tugging on dresses and adjusting bouquets.

Grandma Sperling stopped when she got to me. "You look nice with a little makeup on your face." She even smiled a little.

"Thanks," I said. "Sam did it."

Bob's brother Rick walked over to us. He looked kind of stiff in that black tux with the white flower pinned to the jacket. "Are the mothers ready to be seated?" he asked in a low voice.

"I think we are," Bob's mother said as she and Grandma Sperling made their way to the front of the line. Rick would escort Bob's mother to one of the front row seats and Grandma Sperling to the other. Then the wedding would start.

I took a deep breath and held my bouquet out in front of me so everyone would think I was into this. I was not a girl who was worried about her dad and her grandma; I was a bridesmaid in my mom's wedding. I was *happy*. I kept repeating that word to myself inside my head: happy, happy, happy.

All of a sudden, I felt a hand on my arm. I turned and Suzanne gently pulled Sam and me out of the line. She grabbed both our hands and even through the veil I could tell she was trying really hard not to cry, too.

"I just want you both to know how happy I am today," she said, choking on the words. "Bob's a good man, and we're going to have a good life with him."

"I know," Sam said, throwing her arms around her mother.

I just looked down at the floor, because I wasn't part of the "we" she was talking about. But when Suzanne reached out to hug me with her other arm, I let her. Because it was her wedding day.

"Hurry up, Suzanne," one of the other bridesmaids whispered. "Your mom's sitting down."

We all rushed back to our places: Sam and me at the front of the line, Suzanne at the back. And when the violins began to play, Sam and I started down the aisle.

* * *

It was a beautiful wedding. Everyone said so. But when it was over, all I could think was, *I have to get out of here.* Not just out of this church, but out of this town. I couldn't wait until next week. I had to go home. Now. I had to find Joe.

But how was I going to do that in the middle of this big wedding celebration?

After everyone in the whole church hugged Suzanne and Bob and shook hands with me and Sam and the other bridesmaids, we all got into cars and drove to some fancy country club for the dinner and dance. I decided I'd hang around for the dinner. It would be too hard to slip out unnoticed when I was supposed to sit at the big table with Suzanne and Bob and everyone else who'd been in the wedding. But once the lights went down and people started dancing, I wasn't going to hang around.

All I had to do was get to the bus station. In Cedar Rapids. Which was at least thirty miles away. But if I could get there, I could get a bus back home. And once I was home it would be a lot easier to find out what happened to Joe.

Of course, first I had to get back to Suzanne's house so I could get Sherlock. I wasn't going to leave him here. But once I got him, how was I going to get us to Cedar Rapids?

I could call a cab. It would probably take me to Cedar Rapids, but considering how much it had cost me to take a cab to the bus station back home, I might not have enough left for the bus ticket. If I could get Suzanne's purse, I could probably just take the money I needed. But I didn't want to do that. I didn't want to steal from her.

Maybe Sherlock and I could go out to that highway and hitch a ride to Cedar Rapids. But that didn't seem like a great idea, either. I bet even in Iowa bad stuff happened to people who hitchhiked.

While I was wracking my brain for another idea, the band started warming up. Bob slipped off his tux jacket and hung it over the back of his chair, then stood up and reached for Suzanne's hand. As the two of them walked hand in hand to the dance floor, a lightbulb went on inside my head.

I knew exactly how I was going to get to Cedar Rapids.

Chapter Seventeen

I'd seen Bob drop his keys into his inside jacket pocket when we got to the country club. So while everyone else was busy watching Suzanne and Bob glide across the dance floor, I slid over two seats, reached into his inside pocket, and pulled out the keys. I wasn't entirely sure Bob had a key to Suzanne's house, but now that the two of them were married, I thought the odds were pretty good.

My plan was to drive Bob's car to Suzanne's house, pick up my dog and my stuff, and then drive myself to the Cedar Rapids bus station and leave Bob's car there. Assuming I could find the bus station. There would probably be signs, though. If I was lucky, there would be a bus heading north tonight and I could still get on it, even if I had to switch to another bus in some other town to get all the way to the Twin Cities. If I was *really* lucky, I'd be out of Clearwater before Suzanne even realized I was gone.

"What are you doing way over there?" Sam asked, sliding over to me.

I tucked the hand with Bob's keys underneath the skirt of my dress. I wasn't sure whether she'd seen me grab them or not. "I couldn't see from over there," I said quickly. Which wasn't exactly a lie. The dance floor was at the opposite end of the room from where we were, so most of the rest of the wedding party had gotten up and moved closer to the dance floor. Sam and I were the only ones left at our table.

Sam scooted her chair back. "Well, why don't we move closer then?"

"Okay," I said. This was actually a time when having a purse would have come in handy. Sam had a little silver purse that she'd borrowed from Suzanne, but I'd told them I didn't need one. And now I had no place to hide the keys.

As Sam and I stood at the edge of the crowd in our matching hot pink, I folded my arms across my chest and hid Bob's keys between my elbow and my side. By now Grandma and Grandpa Sperling had joined Suzanne and Bob on the dance floor, and one of Bob's brothers was leading their mother onto the floor.

"You guys can go out and dance, too, you know," Paula said when she noticed Sam and me standing there. "Anyone in the immediate family can go out."

"Really?" Sam said. She looked at me hopefully. "Do you want to?"

"I don't know. It's a slow song. Don't you think it would be weird to dance with each other to a slow song?"

Sam's face fell. "Yeah. I guess."

"How about dancing with me?" one of Bob's brothers asked. He slapped another groomsman on the arm with the back of his hand. "And I'll bet Dan would be willing to dance, too."

Dan turned around. "Sure. Which one of you lovely ladies would like to dance with me?" He held out his hand to both of us.

"You go ahead," I told Sam. "I just want to watch."

Sam looked disappointed. "You're not going to come?"

"Not right now," I said, squeezing Bob's keys.

I stayed where I was and watched them all for a few seconds. Sam and Dan swayed back and forth to the music. So did Grandma and Grandpa Sperling and Bob's brother and mother. But Suzanne and Bob danced like they actually knew what they were doing. Suzanne had the train of her dress pinned up behind her and they seemed to be dancing real dance steps. They looked so…elegant moving around the floor together. So *perfect.*

When the slow song ended, the band launched into a faster song with a pounding beat and a bunch of people went out to join them on the dance floor. I waited to make sure Sam was going to stay where she was. She caught me looking at her and motioned for me to come over and dance with her, but I shook my head. I'm not sure she even saw because right at that second Dan started spinning her faster and faster around the floor. She laughed as the skirt of her dress billowed out around her.

Everybody in the room was either dancing, watching people who were dancing, or talking amongst themselves.

I slowly made my way to the door, trying not to draw attention to myself. But even if anyone saw me, they probably thought I was just going to the bathroom. I paused at the door long enough to glance over at Sam one more time. For about three seconds I wondered if I was doing the right thing. Sam and I were just starting to get to know each other and now I was going to leave?

But I had to. I had to find Joe.

I would write Suzanne and Sam a note when I picked up Sherlock, so they wouldn't worry. I'd tell them my grandma had a stroke and was in the hospital and that was why I had to go home. They'd understand. It wasn't like anyone actually needed me here. It was Suzanne's wedding night.

Clutching Bob's keys, I hurried through the lobby, out the door, and across the parking lot. It wasn't easy to run in a bridesmaid's dress and fancy shoes. When I got to Bob's car, I tried the door. Locked. Just like I would have expected. There was no automatic door opener on Bob's key ring, so I sure hoped one of these keys would unlock his car. I started sticking random keys into the lock until one finally turned. As I lifted the door handle to get in, I heard a voice call across the parking lot, "T.J.! What are you doing?"

It was Sam, and she was coming toward me.

I quick got in Bob's car, slammed the door closed, and wiggled the key into the ignition. But my hand was shaking so bad I couldn't get the car started.

She pounded on the window. "What are you doing? You can't take Bob's car!" she yelled as the motor turned over.

Yes, I can. I put the car in reverse and started to back up, but Sam ran around behind the car.

"Jeez Louise!" I cried, slamming my foot on the brake. I put the car back in park and rolled down my window. I could still hear the dance music from out here. "Are you trying to get yourself killed?" I asked, sticking my head out the window.

"Are you?" she shot back. "You can't drive!"

"I already told you I can. Now get out of my way."

"No!" She pressed herself up against the back end of the car as though she could somehow physically prevent the car from moving. "Where are you going, anyway?"

I did not have time for this. "I can't tell you."

"You can't tell me, but wherever it is, it's important enough to steal a car to get there?"

"I'm not stealing it," I said. "I'm borrowing it. Bob will get it back when I'm done. Now will you please move? And whatever you do, don't tell your mom about this!"

"Why not?" she asked in the most determined voice I'd ever heard from her. "Give me one good reason why I shouldn't tell her."

"Because sisters don't tattle on each other," I said. I thought that would get her. She was the one who was all excited about us being sisters.

"Sisters also don't keep secrets from each other," Sam countered. "Didn't we promise that we would always tell each other the truth about everything?"

Technically, yes. But I had crossed my fingers when we made that promise.

"Can I come with you?" she asked.

"What? No!" Even if I wanted to, I couldn't take her with me. Not to Cedar Rapids. Certainly not to the Twin Cities.

"Then tell me what's going on."

It was obvious I wasn't getting out of here until I did. So I motioned for her to come over to my window.

She narrowed her eyes. "How do I know you won't just whip out of this parking lot if I move away from the back of the car?"

I had to admit the thought had crossed my mind. But I knew if I did that, she'd just run right inside and tell her mom and I wouldn't even make it back to her house, much less all the way to Cedar Rapids.

I had to tell her something.

"I promise I'm not going to leave," I said. "I just don't want to keep shouting, okay? So please, come over here."

She looked like she wasn't sure she could trust me, but she came over. I saw she had a big dirt smudge on the front of her dress. "Okay," she said, leaning her elbows on my open window. "Where are you going?"

"I'm going home."

Her eyes grew wide. "You're going to drive Bob's car all the way to Minnesota?"

"No. I'm just driving to the bus station in Cedar Rapids. I'll take a bus the rest of the way."

"But why do you have to go home now? I thought you liked us."

"I do," I said, lowering my eyes. "But my grandma's sick. She had another stroke and she's in the hospital. She might not make it. That's why I have to go." *The best lies have an element of truth to them.*

"Well, why is that such a big secret? If you tell my mom, she'll drive you to the bus station. In fact, she and Bob might even drive you all the way home."

"I don't want them to. Not tonight. It's their wedding night. I'll leave her a note. At your house. I have to go there to pick up my stuff anyway. But I really have to go."

I could see she was working that over in her brain, but I couldn't tell whether she believed me or not.

"Okay," she said, backing away from the car. "Then...I guess this is good-bye."

"Yeah," I said as a hollow spot opened in my chest.

"Please don't tell them you saw me leave," I said. "Not yet."

She didn't answer. She just turned around and slowly started walking toward the country club.

Part of me wanted to call her back and say, *Wait! I changed my mind. I want you to come with me.* But that would have been crazy. And part of me wanted to forget about Joe and go back inside with Sam. But I hardly knew these people. They weren't my family. Joe was my family and I had to find out what was going on. I put the car in reverse, checked behind me, and slowly backed out.

I was pretty sure I remembered the way to Suzanne's house. It wasn't far. The sun was just starting to go down, so I turned on the headlights. I drove very carefully, making sure to obey every traffic law and keeping my speed five miles below the limit.

As I turned onto Suzanne's street, I heard a police siren.

I checked my rearview mirror. Crap. A police car with flashing lights was right on my tail. He signaled for me to pull over, so I did.

Crap, crap, crap! I was less than two blocks from Suzanne's house. Had I really done something wrong...or had Sam gone back inside and given me away?

I rolled down my window when the police officer came over to my car. "License and registration, please," he said.

"Uh...I don't have them with me," I replied, gripping the steering wheel.

"You're supposed to carry your driver's license and vehicle registration with you at all times," the officer informed me. He stared at me over the tops of his glasses. "Do you even have a driver's license?"

"Of course." I laughed a little.

The officer pulled out a notepad and pen. "I'll need your name, with spelling, and your address, so I can look it up."

He could look it up? "Well, okay. Technically I don't have a driver's license," I admitted. "But I'm a very good driver." Joe always said I was. "In fact, I'm pretty sure I didn't break any laws, so why'd you pull me over?" Joe also said the police couldn't pull you over unless you actually did something wrong.

"It's against the law to drive without a license. It's also against the law to take someone else's vehicle without their permission. Do you have permission to be driving this vehicle right now?"

"Well—"

Just then, another vehicle pulled up behind the police car. A woman in a bride's dress and a man in a tux got out of the backseat and barreled over to us. Suzanne and Bob.

"We'll take it from here, Ken," Bob said. "Thanks."

I slid down in my seat. *I was dead.*

Bob stayed with Ken while Suzanne marched over to me. She yanked open my door. "Slide over," she said coolly. She was MAD.

I lifted myself over the parking brake that separated the two front seats. As I did, my heel caught on the bottom of my dress and I felt the dress rip as I fell into the passenger seat. Great. Just great.

"Let me guess," I muttered as Suzanne buckled herself up. "Sam told on me."

Suzanne didn't answer. She put on the blinker and pulled away from the curb. I turned around in my seat. Suzanne had left her brand new husband standing there in the street, talking to Ken, the police officer.

"Where are we going?" I asked nervously.

"Home to get your stuff. Then to the bus station," Suzanne replied.

Whoa. Not what I expected.

"Are you sure there's a bus to the Twin Cities tonight?" Suzanne asked, her eyes straight ahead.

"I'm...not sure."

"I guess we'll find out when we get there." Sam swung Bob's car into her driveway and reached for her purse, which she'd stashed on the floor. She pulled out a house key and handed it to me.

"You're really going to take me to the bus station? Now?"

"That's what you want, isn't it?"

"Well, I don't expect you to take me there *now*," I said. "Not on your wedding night."

"You don't expect, or even want, much of anything from anybody, do you?"

I wasn't sure what to say to that.

"Your dad told me you were *dead*, T.J.... He attended a memorial service with me. Did you know that? Your dad and your grandparents and our friends and people we didn't even know all sat in a church and had a memorial service for you. But you weren't dead. And your dad knew that. He took you away from me. And he kept you away all this time, until Sam found you. Given all this, I think I've been extremely accommodating. I didn't press charges against Joe. I didn't push for custody, even though I want you to live with Bob, Sam, and me more than anything in the world. All I've asked from you is that you try and get to know us. But you're just not willing to give us a chance."

"No," I said, shifting in my seat. "That's not true." I wanted to get to know them. I really did. I wasn't sure I even realized I wanted to get to know them until right that second, but...I had to get home. I had to find Joe.

"I love you, T.J.," Suzanne said. "More than you will ever know. But I can't force you to love us back. If you want to go home so badly that you would sneak out of my wedding reception and steal a car—"

"No! It's not like that. I don't *want* to go home. I *need* to go home." And then, without even thinking about what I was doing, I told Suzanne everything. Not just about Gram, but about Joe, too. Right there in the front seat of Bob's car.

This time when my eyes filled with tears, I let them come. And for the first time in ten years, I let my mom put her arms around me and hold me. I didn't know what else to do.

Chapter Eighteen

Still in her wedding gown, Suzanne made a bunch of phone calls that night while I sat with Sherlock on the floor of the family room and listened. We found out Gram was in serious, but stable condition. She'd suffered a pretty major stroke and she was sleeping a lot. But she was okay. For now. We also found out Joe had been checked out of the hospital—*he wasn't dead!*—and into a rehab center of some sort. It didn't sound like the same kind of rehab he was in when I went to live with Gram, but he would be there just as long. Eight weeks. Suzanne had the name, address, and phone number of the place.

"Why didn't anybody tell me all this?" I asked, hugging Sherlock to my chest.

"It sounds like your social worker was going to call us on Monday," Suzanne said as she set the phone in her lap.

Why didn't Joe call and tell me himself?

Suzanne came over and sat down on the couch. "I'd like

to know why you didn't tell me right away that your dad was in the hospital," she said.

I looked down at the floor. Did she really want me to say it? *I didn't tell you because I was afraid you'd make me stay with you.*

"You don't have to handle this, or anything else, on your own." She reached for my hand. Her brand new wedding ring sparkled on her finger. "I'm here for you, T.J. Please, let me be here for you."

I didn't even know what she meant by that. What did she think she was going to do? Move into Gram's house with me and help take care of Joe?

"So, what's going to happen to me while Joe's in the rehab center?" I asked. I was almost afraid to hear the answer.

"That's up to you, T.J.," Suzanne said. "You'll always have a home with us. Whenever you want one. But if you want to be closer to your dad and your grandma right now, I...understand."

What? She was going to let me go home? I could tell it wasn't what she wanted, but she would let me do it.

"If you want to go back to the Twin Cities, Mrs. Morris will find a temporary home for you in the Twin Cities," Suzanne added.

"You mean a foster home?" I asked.

"Yes. If you want to go home, we'll have to call your social worker and let her know so she can set something up."

Did I really want to spend the next eight weeks in a foster home?

Well, what was the alternative? Stay here? Away from Joe and Gram? "Can I think about it?" I asked.

"Of course."

"Can I call my dad?"

Suzanne checked her watch. "It's getting a little late, don't you think?"

It was ten after ten. "He might still be awake," I said. I really needed to talk to him.

Suzanne stood up. "All right. I'll go see what everyone else is up to and give you a little privacy."

"Thanks," I said. I knew there were other people in the house. I could hear them talking, but they'd left Suzanne and me alone in the family room.

Once Suzanne left, I picked up the phone and called the Helen O'Neill Rehabilitation Center. I asked to talk to Joseph Wright and the lady who answered the phone didn't say anything about how late it was. She transferred my call and Joe picked up.

"Hello?" He sounded tired, but I didn't care.

"Why didn't you tell me you moved to a different place?"

"T.J.?"

"Why didn't you tell me?" I asked again. It was exactly what Suzanne had asked me less than five minutes ago, but she was much nicer about it with me than I was with Joe.

"You're at Suzanne's," he said, as though not telling me was the most logical thing in the world. "I didn't want Suzanne to know that I was in the hospital."

"No one had to tell Suzanne. You just had to tell me. I didn't know where you were. I was afraid you were dead!"

No response.

I got up and wandered over to the large window, but it was dark outside. I couldn't see anything but my own reflection in the glass. "If you weren't going to tell me you moved to a new place while I was at Suzanne's, when were you going to tell me?" I asked. "When I got back home? Did you think I'd just stay by myself in Gram's house with no money for *eight weeks* while you got better?"

Eight weeks was a long time to stay alone. Even for me.

"I don't know. I guess I didn't think about it."

"You didn't think about it?" I cried. I couldn't believe him!

"You know," I said, anger boiling up inside me, "you're supposed to be the parent here. That means you're supposed to think about these things. You're supposed to think about how the things you do affect other people. Like *me.*"

More silence from Joe.

"I told Suzanne you were in the hospital," I said. "I told Gram, too. In fact, I even told Gram that Sam came to our house three weeks ago and I told her that I was at Suzanne and Sam's house now. Maybe that's why she had another stroke."

No, T.J. It wasn't your fault Gram had a stroke. Gram's old and she's not in very good health. That's what Suzanne had said.

"Did you even know Gram had another stroke?" I asked.

Still nothing.

"Why aren't you saying anything?" I asked.

"I don't know what you want me to say, Teej."

I walked back over to the couch and plopped down. I didn't know what I wanted him to say, either.

"Why did you take me all those years ago, Joe?"

I'd thought he took me because he loved me so much he couldn't stand the idea of Suzanne taking me all the way to Florida.

But was that really love?

Suzanne and Sam thought I was dead all this time. I was beginning to get an idea of what that must have felt like. They lost way more than Joe lost. They lost even more than Joe would have lost if he had just let Suzanne take me to Florida.

And so did I. I lost out on having a regular family.

Joe let out a big breath. "I don't know, T.J. I don't know what to tell you…other than I'm sorry. I'm really sorry."

I couldn't help but wonder what he was sorry about. Was he sorry he'd done all those things or was he sorry he'd gotten caught? Would he ever have told me the truth if Sam hadn't forced him to? Would I ever have known I had a mom and a sister out there?

"I'm not coming home next week," I blurted out. I never even thought about it, I just said it. But now that the words were out…

"You're going to stay with your mom until I'm back home?" Joe asked.

"Yes," I said as my eyes filled with tears again.

You'll always have a home with us, Suzanne had said. *Whenever you want one.*

"And I…I think I may stay longer than that, too."

Joe paused. "How much longer?"

"I don't know," I said. "A while."

* * *

It was late. Well past midnight. But I couldn't sleep.

It wasn't because I was afraid I'd made the wrong decision. It was because I knew I'd made the right one. For everyone. Suzanne had seemed really happy when I told her I was staying. But even so, I still felt like a part of my heart was breaking. Joe and I would see each other again someday and we'd find a way to fix everything that was wrong between us.

But what about Gram? Could I really leave Gram? Especially when she'd just had another stroke? What if I never saw her again? I couldn't think about that. Somehow, I knew Gram would understand. Now that the truth was out, she would want me to know my mom and my sister.

I heard a door open softly down the hall, then a soft tapping on my door.

Suzanne? She and Bob had originally planned to go to a hotel for their wedding night, but after everything that had happened they'd decided to stay here. With me and Sam.

"Come in," I said, sitting up.

The door opened, but it wasn't Suzanne who stuck her head in. It was Sam. Moonlight from my open window shone on her face. "Are you mad at me?" she asked. "For telling my mom you took Bob's car?"

"No," I told Sam. "Not anymore." It was true. I wasn't mad at her about anything anymore.

"Good." Sam came in and sat down beside me on the couch. "I heard about...Joe," she said. "I'm sorry."

I shrugged. "He'll be okay. Eventually." My dog snuggled against both of us.

"Mom also told me you're going to stay with us. That you're even going to go to school here."

School? I hadn't thought about school. But if I was going to stay...I guess I had no choice. "When does it start?"

"Two weeks from Monday," Sam said. "My friends will be so excited. They all want to meet you."

Whoa. It was only the first weekend in August. We didn't start school until after Labor Day in the Twin Cities.

"I'm glad you're going to stay," Sam said, pulling her knees to her chest. "But I want to know something... What would've happened if your dad hadn't gotten hurt? If your dad wasn't in that rehab place, would you still have wanted to stay?"

There were so many *ifs*. What if Gram had never had that first stroke and gone to live at Valley View? What if Sam had never gone searching for Joe? What if Joe had never taken me away? What if Grandpa Sperling had never hit Katie with his car? My life could have been so very different if any one of those things hadn't happened. But things would be different now. That I knew for sure.

"I don't know," I said finally. "Does it really matter? I'm staying. Isn't that what's important?"

Sam thought about it for a minute. "Yeah, I guess so." Then she scratched Sherlock's ears and stood up. "We should get some sleep. Hope you like heavy boxes and lots of stairs. Tomorrow is moving day."

"Right," I said.

Moving day.

And the start of a whole new life.

The End

Also by Dori Hillestad Butler

DO YOU KNOW THE MONKEY MAN?

• 2005 Bank Street College of Education
Teen Book List
• A Scholastic Book Club selection

For thirteen-year-old Samantha, life consists of too many unanswered questions. Why has her father not tried to contact her all these years? How could he have allowed her twin sister to drown in the old Clearwater quarry when they were only three? And how can Samantha's mother expect her to accept some man she hardly knows as her new father? Samantha already has a father out there. Somewhere.

A fateful decision sets into motion a chain of events and confrontations that will change Samantha's and her family's lives forever. As she sets out to find her father and discover what really happened the day her sister was presumed drowned, she uncovers painful secrets that threaten to destroy her family all over again.

Readers will be drawn into Dori Butler's sensitive and suspenseful story of one family's crisis unwittingly brought on by an adolescent girl's search for the truth.

DORI HILLESTAD BUTLER is the author of many works of fiction and nonfiction for young readers. Her middle-grade novel SLIDING INTO HOME has received numerous awards, including an Honor Book Award from the Society of School Librarians International. Butler lives in Coralville, Iowa, with her husband, two sons, a dog, a cat, and a fish named Willie, who keeps her company while she writes. Visit Dori Hillestad Butler's website at *www.kidswriter.com.*